"So, who are you, my lady?" he asked.

Heather laughed.

"Guinevere? Lady Godiva?" Ben continued. "No, I know who you are: you're Titania, queen of the elves."

"That's right."

"And you live in a forest grove filled with sunlight and flowers. And when you walk beneath the trees, a lute player follows and your subjects rush out to touch the hem of your gown."

Heather blushed slightly. "Well, not quite."

"Who are you, then?"

Not *What is your name*, but *Who are you?* Heather didn't know how to answer him. "My name is Heather Scarborough, and I live in Pueblo. Nothing so romantic as what you conjured up, I'm afraid."

His dark eyes sparkled with laughter as he said, "Only because you haven't discovered your destiny yet."

Dear Reader,

Welcome to the Silhouette **Special Edition** experience! With your search for consistently satisfying reading in mind, every month the authors and editors of Silhouette **Special Edition** aim to offer you a stimulating blend of deep emotions and high romance.

The name Silhouette **Special Edition** and the distinctive arch on the cover represent a commitment—a commitment to bring you six sensitive, substantial novels each month. In the pages of a Silhouette **Special Edition**, compelling true-to-life characters face riveting emotional issues—and come out winners. Both celebrated authors and newcomers to the series strive for depth and dimension, vividness and warmth, in writing these stories of living and loving in today's world.

The result, we hope, is romance you can believe in. Deeply emotional, richly romantic, infinitely rewarding—that's the Silhouette **Special Edition** experience. Come share it with us—six times a month!

From all the authors and editors of Silhouette **Special Edition**,

Best wishes,

Leslie Kazanjian,
Senior Editor

RUTH WIND

Strangers on a Train

Silhouette Special Edition

Published by Silhouette Books New York

America's Publisher of Contemporary Romance

To my sister, Retta Catherine,
and my father, James G.,
because they saw what I could not

SILHOUETTE BOOKS
300 East 42nd St., New York, N.Y. 10017

ISBN: 0-373-09555-4

First Silhouette Books printing October 1989

Printed in the U.S.A.

RUTH WIND

has been addicted to books and stories for as long as she can remember. When she realized at the age of seven that some lucky people actually spent their days spinning tales for others, she knew she had found her calling. The precise direction of that calling—romance writing—was decided when she fell in love with the films *Dr. Zhivago* and *Romeo and Juliet*.

The Colorado native holds a bachelor's degree in journalism and lives with her husband and two young sons in a city at the foot of the Rockies.

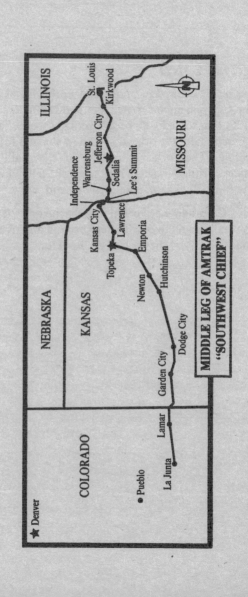

MIDDLE LEG OF AMTRAK "SOUTHWEST CHIEF"

Chapter One

Ben paused between two cars of the train, hearing the small puff of sound in his ears that sometimes signaled an attack—a flashback or a few moments of lost time. It had something to do with the injuries he'd suffered in that last shattering battle—an experience he had never quite been able to piece together in his memory.

He wrapped his fingers securely around a handhold next to the sliding door that led to the passenger car. Fragmentally he thought about trying to get to the safety of a seat. The edges of his vision lit with a soft fur of excruciatingly bright light, and the unwelcome but all-too-familiar sensation of tingling spread through his body.

Looking through the open door of the unmoving train, he focused upon the station with desperate attention, forcing himself to note each tiny detail. It was a small building set against a backdrop of girders and underpinnings that supported the highway. He noted the flat roof and pale bricks of the new station, plopped down like a computer chip into the debris of nineteenth-century industrial-revolution buildings. At the periphery of his vision, bits of flame licked at the furry light. He tightened his hold on the bar and stared at the doorway of the station.

Into the halo of light stepped a woman. For a moment, he thought she was a specter created by his imagination to further confuse the time warp of the scene—one of the ghosts his mind continually conjured up when he was in this state. She emerged from the station with a case in her hand, into the gray light of the dark, fall day, in a gloom made denser by the St. Louis air. She was neither small nor particularly tall, and a long black coat hid her figure to below her knees. But Ben was transfixed, unable to decide whether she was real or a vision.

She had yards of golden hair spilling over the black velveteen coat; it cascaded over her shoulders and down her arms and back, falling well past her waist. The crown was woven into what seemed to be a series of braids, worn like a cap.

He continued to stare as she moved toward the train, mesmerized by the fantastic beauty of that hair. As she drew closer, his gaze lit upon her face, an oval as pale as the overcast sky, unremarkable except for the eyes, which were a very dark blue. There was something distinctly medieval about her and he knew she had to be a phantom created by his seizure, even when she climbed the stairs and the details of her personage grew more and more definite. "Titania," he breathed.

"Pardon me?" she replied, staring, startled, into his face.

Real then, he thought, and blinked, struggling to control the interruptions of the nerve signals in his brain. When he looked at her, the blue eyes showed alarm, and the spun-gold splendor of her hair blended with the halo of light in his eyes. She looked like a heroine in the late show, leaving him speechless.

A little rush of receding blood in his face told him it would be over in a moment. Not long now. He closed his eyes, lurching as the train chugged into motion, his foot and ankle refusing to support him. He stumbled, and the woman steadied him with a gesture of firm kindness. "Thank you," he said thickly. He braced himself against the wall. He didn't look at her as he told her, "I'll be all right now."

"Are you sure?" She dipped her head to look into his face. "I can help you to your seat."

"I'm okay." The words were slurry even in his own ears and he glanced away from the probe of her eyes, knowing he sounded drunk.

She gave a quick, curt nod and eased by him, her body unavoidably brushing against his as she struggled with the case in her hand. The door slid shut behind her.

Ben took long, deep breaths of the cold air that whipped into the tiny area. Slowly his brain ceased its rebellion. It took longer for the trembling of his limbs to steady. His hands would shake perceptibly until he slept tonight.

Feeling winded, he straightened, remembering the woman. God, was she real? He looked over his shoulder, almost afraid to discover that she was.

Heather found a seat near the back of the underfilled car and struggled with her guitar case and canvas shoulder bag until it was as out of the way as she could manage. She took the window seat and settled herself against the comfortable cushions. She sighed, trying to shake her mood.

For a moment out there, she'd been painfully reminded of James. Although he was so drunk he could barely stand, that man between the cars had made her think of James with an ache of longing she hadn't felt in a long time.

It wasn't surprising. Everything the last few days had brought James with it. It was periodic, her grief, triggered by the most mundane daily occurrences—a laugh in the back of the theater, a pair of boots like those he had worn, a car he would have noticed. Now drunks on trains twisted the knife. She pressed her lips together and stared at the backs of the red brick buildings they passed as the train picked up speed.

She was tired. The trips to her mother's house always had to be rushed—twenty-four hours on the train to get to St. Louis, twenty-four to get back to Pueblo, with a long weekend sandwiched in between. This time, Heather had stayed three days. It was the longest she could stand to be under her mother's roof. Even as a child, the great booming stillness of the St. Louis home had made her feel claustrophobic. Now that her mother lived alone, mostly dreaming of the departed faces that had once filled her hours, Heather felt the house to be more than ever like a mausoleum. It was so quiet, the ticking of the clocks could be heard at any hour of the day.

Heather shrugged unconsciously. No wonder she had been thinking so often of James again, the way death shrouded everything in that house—not just human death, but death of time and of joy, as well. Her mother even rebelled at putting a recording of Rachmaninoff on the stereo.

She leaned back against the seat and closed her eyes. After three years, she'd thought the sorrow ought to be finished. At twenty-nine, she was far too young to mourn for the rest of her life. Intellectually she knew that. Emotionally—well, emotionally, it was more difficult. No other man could take James's place. Not ever.

"Excuse me." A voice interrupted her thoughts—a male voice with the blurry undertones of the West.

Heather opened her eyes. Standing in the aisle next to her seat, holding his soft, brushed Stetson in his hands, was the drunk from the landing. "Yes?" she asked warily. All she needed was a drunk to keep her company all the way to Kansas City.

"Can I sit down for a minute?"

He didn't sound drunk now. Nor did he look it. She measured him for a moment. He had a kind face, she observed, and wondered what it was that made a face look kind. It was the eyes, she decided—eyes the color of a cup of rich, black coffee, and fringed with the sort of sweeping lashes women always wish for and certain lucky men end up with. A thick mustache, threaded with red and blond amid the more predominant brown, framed a full bottom lip and square chin. He looked nothing like James, she thought, and frowned before she nodded to him.

The man swung himself into the seat opposite Heather and folded his hands loosely between his knees. "I wanted to apologize."

She held herself stiffly erect, wanting to maintain distance. His hair was cut neatly around his face, but loose brown waves fell well over his collar. Heather bit her lip—*nothing like James*. What had made her think that? James had been blond and aristocratic looking and blessed with the bone structure of a prince. "What apology could you owe me?" she asked.

He cleared his throat before he spoke. "I frightened you, and I'm sorry." His gazed settled on her. "I've got a little trouble with the nerves in my brain. Things get kind of mixed up—almost like I'm dreaming. I'm sure you thought I was some crazy drunk, and

I wanted to let you know you don't have to be afraid of me."

Heather stared at him, surprised at this straightforwardness. "I *did* think you were drunk. I'm sorry."

"It's natural."

His warm gaze stayed locked on her face, uncommonly direct. Heather glanced at her hands.

"You have the prettiest hair I think I've ever seen," he drawled.

Heather looked at him. A grin danced over the rugged face and for a moment, she couldn't reply, amazed at the transformation that smile made on his face. All the lines fell into place, his irises lit with mischief and his mouth curved broadly, openly, as if laughter was what it was meant for. Without thinking, she said, "You're very handsome when you smile."

A chuckle escaped those laughing lips. "Does that mean I could ask you to have a cup of coffee with me?" She hesitated, suddenly aware that his hands were trembling. Handsome or not, she had no business relaxing in the company of a total stranger. She preferred formal introductions, made by acquaintances of long standing. *That's your city upbringing*, she told herself.

"If you're worried about another seizure," he assured her, his smile fading, "I can assure you there won't be another one."

His honesty touched her. What must it be like to know you might suddenly lose control in public at any moment? "You don't have to tell me all of this."

"I know." Still his eyes met hers evenly.

Heather couldn't have said why, but she suddenly agreed to his offer. "I could really use a cup of coffee," she said. What, after all, could happen on a train, in the company of so many other people?

"Great." He stood up. Heather found herself admiring his long, hard thighs encased in close-fitting jeans. Her eyes flickered up to his face to see that smile again, a smile that said he'd noticed her perusal and was pleased by it. She felt her ears tingle with embarrassment and stood quickly.

His hand, inserted between the rack above the seats and her head, was all that saved her from a nasty blow. "Don't get all flustered, now," he admonished, with a teasing note in his voice.

The tingle of self-consciousness spread from her ears over her cheeks. She was flustered beyond explanation. To make matters worse, as she tried to recover herself and move into the aisle, she felt a length of her hair catch in one of the buttons of his jacket. She winced. "I knew I should have braided it," she muttered.

He reached up to untangle the snagged tendril of hair. "I'm glad you didn't."

Up close, he smelled of leather and cigarettes—an overwhelmingly male scent. Heather risked a glance at him as he freed her hair. He was utterly masculine, she thought: coarse skin and booted feet, a slightly bow-legged stance. Had he ridden in rodeos? Was that where he'd received his injury? She mentally shook her head. How did she even know he'd been injured? Maybe it was an accident at birth or an inborn condition. Somehow, though, she didn't think so.

She straightened as he pulled the last of her hair free. One long golden strand still clung to his coat, and he wound it tightly around the button. "According to some voodoo spells, this one little piece of hair could give me a whole lot of power over you," he said.

"I suppose," Heather replied, recovering a little of her equilibrium, "that I'll have to trust you not to use it."

He inclined his head and lifted an eyebrow, saying nothing. Then he turned to lead the way to the café car.

Heather walked behind him. His progress was slow, careful. He had a definite limp and a lack of mobility in his left leg, giving credence to the theory of an injury. Strangely, the limp wasn't as ungainly as it might have been. He moved his body with it rather than against it, as though it had been with him a long time. Other than the limp, there was nothing at all wrong with the back view of him. The long legs, encased in new blue jeans, led to a torso that tapered attractively from wide shoulders. He'd slapped his hat back on, and the dark waves of his hair curled appealingly over his collar.

She lowered her eyes, working her hand into a firmer grip on the guitar case she carried. It had been a long time since any man had stirred more than a cursory interest in her. She rarely even noticed men. Surely there was no danger in admiring a fellow traveler, she thought, taking another peek at the broad shoulders. The circumstances prevented the possibility of anything coming of it.

In the café car, they paused at the counter. "What would you like?" her companion asked Heather.

"Oh, coffee is fine."

"No yogurt? An orange?"

Heather smiled. "No, thank you. My mother always makes certain I'm well fed before I begin my journey home."

"Visiting your mother," he said. "Is that what you've been doing?"

She nodded. But his attention had shifted, ordering cups of coffee for each of them and a sweet roll for himself. He hesitated very briefly upon looking at the coffee cups, and Heather smoothly picked up both. "If you would be so kind as to carry my guitar..." she said graciously, and led the way to a booth.

When they'd settled, he poured several packets of sugar and cream into his coffee. At Heather's expression of amazement, he responded, "When I was injured, I had to give up drinking. Seems like ever since then, I can't get enough sugar. I figure," he went on licking one finger, "sugar won't kill me."

"And liquor?"

"Liquor wouldn't have killed me either." Again that engaging grin flashed on his face. "It was the fights I started when I was drinking that would've done that."

"What did you fight about?"

"Anything. The color of the sky, the size of a tree, a brand of beer. Didn't matter."

She smiled a little, as she was meant to, and sipped gingerly at the hot coffee.

He ate his sweet roll with relish, saying not a word until it was done. Afterward, he carefully brushed his mustache clean with his napkin and leaned forward, elbows on the table, to stare at Heather. "So, who are you, my lady? Guinevere? Lady Godiva?"

She laughed.

"No, I know who you are. You're Titania, the queen of the elves."

That's right."

"And you live in a forest grove, filled with sunlight and flowers. And when you walk beneath the trees, a lute player follows and your subjects rush out to touch the hem of your gown."

Heather blushed slightly. "Well, not quite."

"Who are you, then?"

Not "what is your name," but "who are you?" Heather didn't know how to answer him. "My name is Heather Scarborough and I live in Pueblo. Nothing so romantic as what you conjured up, I'm afraid."

"Only because—" and now his eyes definitely sparkled with laughter "—you haven't discovered your destiny."

Heather laughed out loud. The sound surprised her as it rolled up from her chest. It felt good, like a pleasure just dimly remembered. "You might be right." Shaking her hair back from her face, she looked at him. "And you? Are you a refugee from the OK Corral, maybe, or the James Gang?"

He grinned. "Close. Real close." He laughed at some secret joke and extended his hand. "My name is Ben Shaw."

Heather held out her own hand. His strong fingers clasped hers gently. Instead of shaking it as she'd expected, he drew her hand forward and planted a kiss on her knuckles. His lips were firm and warm, and his mustache tickled her skin. Her hand had been kissed before, but she felt this one clear to her toes, in a zingy rush of sensation. Hastily she drew her hand back. The imprint lingered like a ghost and she found she'd lost her voice.

Ben filled the pause. "So, your mother lives in St. Louis?"

"Yes." The word came out on a sigh.

"You don't like visiting your mother?"

Heather shook her head slowly. "I hate to admit it." In fact, she'd never done so to anyone before. "I love her, but she's grown into a bitter old woman, and it's hard to be around her."

"What makes her bitter?"

"I don't know, exactly. She misses my father. He died two and half years ago." Almost six months to the day after James, she remembered with a pang.

What a year that had been. "I understand why she misses him. I just wish she would find something to do with her time."

"How old is she?"

"Seventy."

His mouth turned down at the corners in surprise. "You must have been an afterthought."

Heather smiled slightly. "Yes. They never thought they'd have children. I was born when my mother was thirty-nine. My father was forty-three."

"Only child?"

She nodded.

Ben's eyes narrowed thoughtfully. "A lonely child, too, with aging parents and no brothers or sisters. I bet you read a lot of books."

She cocked her head, unsure how she felt about this acute perception. A part of her resented the intrusion. Another part of her felt so relaxed with him it was difficult to work up the defenses necessary to keep him at arm's length. "I read a lot." Her gaze fell on his hands just as he lifted one to grasp his coffee. Again the trembling of the fingers struck her. "Do you mind if I ask how you were injured?"

He shook his head. For a moment he concentrated on the coffee cup in front of him and Heather realized she'd been unpardonably rude. "I'm sorry," she said quickly. "Please ignore my bad manners."

"It's all right."

When he lifted those sweeping lashes, there was an echo of James in his eyes—and she understood. Before he could continue, Heather stated flatly, "Vietnam." There was utter certainty in her words.

"Good guess."

She looked out the window at the farmland they were passing, a landscape that dripped greenery in the summertime. As Heather looked at it now, the gray sky and withered growth seemed to reflect the sudden bleakness in her heart. It seemed as though every man she met was a veteran, she thought bitterly. Not terribly surprising, considering that Pueblo boasted some staggering statistics on numbers of former soldiers of the Vietnam War. Her adopted hometown was a working-class city, traditional and patriotic. The boys of the era had served their country even in that unpopular war, and if Heather's experience was any indication, many had lived to regret it—if they lived at all. "It wasn't a guess," she admitted quietly.

Ben remained silent for a minute. "Sore spot?"

Heather gathered herself and looked at him. It certainly wasn't his fault, and obviously he'd paid a high price himself. "My husband was a Vietnam veteran. He used to say you could tell a man who'd seen action by a look in their eyes."

"You're a widow, I take it?"

She inclined her head. "You take it right."

"I'm sorry."

Heather met his eyes. Again the kindness of his eyes warmed her. He wasn't merely mouthing polite sympathy. "So am I."

A pause fell between them and Heather drank the last of her coffee. "I have some studying to do," she said finally, reaching for her guitar. "It was a pleasure to meet you."

Ben stood with her, blocking her exit. His chin was level with her eyes. "You don't have to run off, Heather. I think I frightened you again." He grasped her upper arm in a gesture of comfort.

The moment he touched her, some of the panic she had indeed been feeling slipped away. For the smallest wisp of a breath, she studied his face again, uncertain what the next seconds would bring.

He made no move toward her, but he didn't release her arm. "Sit down. I'm not crazy or haunted. I've got a gimpy leg and a brain that kicks out from time to time, but you're safe with me. I promise."

What he said wasn't true. He *was* haunted. Behind that easy laughter and gentle teasing, there was another man. Perhaps that was why she sat back down. Simple curiosity compelled her to find out what lay beneath the kind facade—if anything.

He dropped his arm to his side. "Now, tell me, are you running machine guns for the IRA, or is that really a guitar?"

She laughed. "You have an overly active imagination. Do I look like the type to run guns?"

"You never know. I hear they use the sweetest faces of all."

"It's a guitar, I promise."

"What do you play? Bluegrass?" he asked in mock hope.

"Sorry. Classical."

"Ah. Is that what you do to earn a living?"

"Some. I teach guitar classes and do background for a Shakespearean troupe."

"Are you an actress?"

"Sort of. It chose me, rather than the other way around." She shrugged. "I do a lot of Shakespeare, more because I look right for the era than anything else, I think."

"Well, you do look right." He grinned. "I didn't think you were real when I first saw you."

"What did you think I was—a ghost?"

"Something like that." He looked at their empty cups. "You want another cup? I'm going to get myself one."

Heather nodded. "Sure."

He stood. "Why don't you take off your coat and stay awhile?"

She hadn't realized she was still bundled up in the heavy coat. It was like a shield of armor in the city. Obligingly she shrugged it off.

At the counter, Ben turned to look at her as she removed her coat. Below it, she wore a soft white blouse with full sleeves. One long tendril of blond hair trailed over her shoulder and the small rise of her breast to disappear below the line of the table. She was real, all right, he thought—though what the hell he was doing with her, he sure didn't know. She definitely wasn't the kind of woman he generally kept company with. Nothing about her suggested those lusty, hard-living females—the kind of women who asked nothing of him and didn't probe.

He shook his head. He'd spent a lot of years hiding after the war; hiding until he'd almost lost sight of everything he was. One morning he'd awakened to find half his life gone, and he'd vowed not to waste another day. This woman, for whatever amount of time he could sit with her, was who he wanted now. She might not be his type. He grinned to himself. But then again, she might be more his type than anyone he'd ever met.

Carefully he carried the cups back to the table. Inevitably a little sloshed onto his fingers and he licked the place with a rueful smile at Heather.

She smiled back. "I would have helped."

"I'm used to it. No big deal. Usually I make sure there's a saucer." His gaze flickered out to the cleared fields beyond the windows. "You know, the first time I saw this view, the trees and everything had about a quarter inch of ice on them. The sun was shining and that ice glittered in every color of the rainbow. I had never seen anything like it." He grinned at her. "I acted like a little kid, grabbing everybody to get them to look at it."

Heather laughed. "And anyone who was raised around here thought you were crazy."

"Yep. They knew how cold it had to be to make it look like that." He shook his head in wonder. "Still, it's a good memory. The West doesn't ever look like that. No water in the air.''

"I like Western winters," Heather said. Weather seemed a safe topic. "It's so cold in St. Louis you can't go anywhere without a floor-length coat and mittens and a hat.''

Ben sipped his coffee and smiled his encouragement.

"I came to Pueblo to go to school, and the first winter I spent there, they had a cold snap in January. The temperature dropped to about ten below. I kept hearing the reports, and I was afraid to go out, thinking it would be like St. Louis. It wasn't." She smiled. "I even took a walk.''

"Do you like the summers? Pueblo's pretty hot.''

Heather laughed. "I have the freedom of arranging my own schedule, so I just turn on the air conditioner and go to sleep in the hottest part of the day. By the time I wake up, the heat's bearable.''

"Ah, now that's intelligence—a siesta.''

"You may as well sleep." She shifted forward in her seat. "Have you ever noticed how people move on those really hot days? They drift through the afternoons like they have a ten-pound weight on each foot." She realized she was leaning over the table, and a sudden attack of shyness washed through her. He was a good listener, she thought; able to start conversations and keep them going with only a few little comments of his own. She was astonished to realize that she still knew next to nothing about him.

"You're blushing, Titania."

"It's the only time I ever have any color in my face," she said self-depreciatively. "I like to turn it on every so often."

He laughed and touched her hand lightly.

A tall, graying man paused by the table. "Ben! Hey, old man, I thought that was you."

Ben swiveled to glance up. "George! How the hell are you?" He stuck out his hand and the other man shook it. "Where are you headed?"

"San Francisco to see my sister."

"Is your wife with you?"

He nodded and sat down as Ben made room for him. Although the man looked pointedly at Heather, Ben made no move to introduce her. The two men chatted about people Heather naturally knew nothing of, and after a few minutes, when the conversation showed no signs of slowing, she cleared her throat delicately.

"Thank you for the coffee, Ben," she said, and stood. "I really do have some studying to do."

George didn't get up, and an expression of irritation crossed Ben's face. Awkwardly, he half rose around the table. "It was a pleasure meeting you, Heather."

"You, too," she answered vaguely, and smiled. Then there was nothing left to do but return to the passenger cars and her seat.

Ben glanced at George as Heather left. "Damn, man, you want to give me a little air, here?"

George laughed. "Sure. She one of your fans?"

So, Ben realized, George had imagined himself to be doing a good deed, rescuing him from a fan who had cornered him. The reverse was true, he thought wryly. Maybe it was better this way. He couldn't for the life of him see how that delicate woman would ever understand all that he was, all that he'd done and gone through. He didn't see how her frailty and quiet interests would fit into his life.

"No," he said, finally. "I just met her and thought she was pretty."

"Not exactly your type, is she?"

Ben shook his head, conscious of a tinge of regret. "No. Guess not."

Chapter Two

The claim to have some studying to do was only half true, Heather reflected as she returned to her seat. The small theatrical company to which she belonged was in rehearsal for a production of *Twelfth Night*. That part was true. The rest—well, she knew the music inside out, for she'd composed most of it herself.

Still, needing to add some credence to her claim, she dutifully pulled out her paperback edition of the play and began to recite the lines quietly to herself. Then she closed the book and recreated the scenes in her mind as they would appear on Friday night. After a time, the rocking motion of the train lulled her into a light doze. It was dusk when she awoke, and an elderly woman had taken the seat opposite Heather.

Heather stared out at the graying scenery, vaguely disoriented. James had walked through her dreams again, laughing. It was a sound she'd always heard when they were in the company of other people, rarely when they were alone. The jovial front he erected in social situations exhausted him, and when they returned home, more often that not he would stare moodily at the television or restlessly pace their small house, resisting all of Heather's attempts to engage him in conversation.

She sighed. When dreams of him haunted her, she always awoke with conflicting emotions: the all-pervasive guilt, and relief. The relief fed the guilt, and guilt renewed the grief in a cycle Heather thought would never end.

There were other widows who didn't linger so long in the limbo of mourning. She'd seen women begin to date again after six months, sometimes getting involved too quickly, in an effort to find lost intimacy again. Well, Heather thought with a droll twist to her mouth, she hadn't made that mistake.

No other man had appealed to her since James had died. Unbidden, a picture of Ben Shaw flickered through her imagination. Just as quickly, Heather brushed it away. If a man had done time in Vietnam—especially if he'd been injured and carried that echo of jungle war in his eyes—she wasn't the right woman for him. James had taught her that. She simply wasn't strong enough to understand the demons a sensitive man could carry.

It wasn't that she felt all veterans were slightly a-tilt. She knew many people had served in that war in much the same manner as any other—it had just been Heather's luck to get mixed up with one who didn't, who spent the rest of his short life reliving war scenes, trying to undo the damage he felt he had done. James had wanted to be a priest when he was seventeen. Instead, he'd been drafted. At first it had seemed odd to her that he hadn't taken conscientious objector's status, given his religious feelings. But time had shown him to be as patriotic as the rest of Pueblo, and he'd felt he would shame his family and his country by becoming a C.O.

With a sigh of annoyance, Heather shifted. She wished she could play her guitar, but it wasn't polite to fill any small space with more noise than was utterly necessary.

"Excuse me, honey," said the elderly woman in the other seat.

Heather looked at her inquiringly. The woman was doing some sort of needlework and she held a pattern out to Heather, pointing with a gnarled finger to a spot circled in red.

"I can't make out the code there in this light. Could you tell me what number that is?"

"Of course." Heather smiled and took the piece of paper. "It's an eight."

"Thank you. I ought to put it away, I suppose. But I'm going to Utah to see my new grandchild and I wanted to get it finished."

It was a cross-stitch pattern of little bears and balloons. "It's beautiful. Was the baby a boy or a girl?"

"A little girl," she answered with a proud smile. "The first daughter of a first daughter of a first daughter."

"How wonderful!" Heather exclaimed with sincerity.

"Do you have children of your own?"

"No, I don't."

"Are you one of those career women?" she asked suspiciously.

Heather laughed lightly. Only an elderly woman from the Heartland could have asked that question in that tone of voice without getting a bristling response. Being the traditional hearth-warmer and having gained satisfaction and joy from her life, this woman saw it as her duty to perpetuate the family and tradition, hardly viewing full-time motherhood as the outmoded calling many thought it to be. Heather had seem many of her ilk in Pueblo. "In a way. I'm a musician. But I'm also a widow."

"Ah," she said, peering at Heather over her smart, gold-rimmed glasses. "I thought there was something sad about you. Has he been gone long?"

"Three years, November ninth."

"Oh... Coming up on an anniversary is always hard. I'm fine until my husband's comes up, but plooey—" she made a sweeping gesture with her hand "—then I'm a basket case for a few weeks."

"I always feel like I'm being melodramatic."

"Heavens, no. It's perfectly natural. It'll probably be better once you get yourself another husband and some babies, though."

Heather grinned. "You might be right."

"What kind of musician are you?"

"Guitarist. I compose and play classical music."

"I like guitar music. It's soothing."

"Yes."

"My name is Madeline Gordon," the woman said, almost as an afterthought.

Heather told her hers, then the conversation lapsed into silence as small talk between strangers will do. Heather looked out the window to the points of light twinkling on in farmhouses along the route. For a moment, she allowed herself to imagine the luxury of living in a home, with the noisy voices of children and steamy windows at dinnertime, and a husband coming home to a meal she'd lovingly prepared. She thought she would like it, would like to create a home for a family. She let the vision expand a little. There would be soft pillows on the living room couch and toys scattered underfoot, maybe a big dog hovering about the corners of the kitchen, licking his chops in anticipation of supper scraps. Love and chaos. And Heather in the middle of it all—mother and wife and housekeeper.

It was a vision so completely different from that of her own silent, ordered childhood, she had to wonder if it even existed outside scripts written for television. Comforting to imagine, though, she thought. What

sort of man would complete the picture? She had no
clear idea—just someone tall and kind and full of
honest laughter.

With a small smile for her indulgence, Heather returned her attention to the older woman. They had
dinner together in the little café car, eating hamburg-
ers and drinking coffee to chase away the chill of the
drafty railway car. Heather glimpsed Ben once, asleep
in one of the other passenger sections, his hat cradled
on his chest. With surprise, she found she was disappointed he hadn't sought her out again. She deliberately turned her eyes away from the sleeping face.
Whatever man she'd imagined for her farmhouse, it
wouldn't be some stranger she met on a train.

The elderly woman slept during the last leg of the
journey into Kansas City, where an hour-long layover
was scheduled at midnight. Heather read a magazine
and dozed, anxious now for her private little room on
the train that would take her into La Junta tomorrow
afternoon. In the roomette she could play her guitar
all night if she wished, watching the Kansas fields
sweep by.

The Kansas City station had always intrigued
Heather. One portion of the huge building had been
improved with modern wall-coverings and escalators
and a new magazine shop. It was in this section that
passengers awaited the next train.

Outside the renovated area, however, stretched the
cavernous halls of the old railway station, and walk-

ing through it, Heather never failed to feel the past swirling around her. She could almost touch the women in their velvet dresses and corsets and bustles. It wasn't difficult to imagine the ladies' plumed hats and gentlemen with pocket watches in the hallway of the past.

When Mrs. Gordon spoke it was a surprise. "This part of the station always frightens me," said the elderly woman. "It's old and creepy."

Heather took her hand and looped it through her arm with a reassuring pat. "Stick with me, madam," she said lightly in an imitation of an English accent. "I'll see you come to no harm."

Mrs. Gordon laughed nervously. "Thank you, dear."

She saw the old woman settled with a magazine and excused herself to brush her hair. She wove it into one long braid that touched the swell of her hips, then slipped the braid under her coat. Finally she pulled a black tam over her head. The effect was what she'd wished for. No one would notice her in any crowd without her hair. It was her only beauty—the only distinction she had with her pale skin and slight figure; and if she were honest with herself, this was one of the reasons she couldn't bear to part with it.

The other, stronger reason had nothing to do with vanity. She'd once read that women felt one of two ways about their hair—either they wore it as an accessory to be changed with the seasons and fashions, or they thought of it as an extension of themselves, like a limb. Heather would no more chop off her hair than cut off a toe. It was unthinkable.

But in the strange confines of an Amtrak station in an unfamiliar city, it was best to remain unnoticed.

She rejoined Mrs. Gordon, who gasped at Heather's transformation. "You look about thirteen," she commented.

Heather laughed. "Since I'm more than a decade and a half past that, I thank you. I think." She scanned the room curiously. No sign of Ben Shaw. Perhaps Kansas City had been his destination, she thought. This hadn't occurred to her until then, and she realized she'd been hoping to run into him tomorrow, perhaps in the dining or the observation car. She chided herself as being ridiculous now.

"How about if I find us something to drink?" Heather suggested.

"That would be nice. If it's coffee, I take it black."

Heather nodded at the hint. She headed for the little news store. On her last trip through, there'd been coffee in there. As she rounded the corner into the shop, she noticed a large urn on a table, with Styrofoam cups, baskets of creamers, sugar, and tea bags. Heather headed for it.

A body appeared between the table and herself, and she looked up into Ben Shaw's dark eyes. "I hardly recognized you in that getup," he drawled. He folded his arms over his chest. "Come to think of it, I never did see that guitar. You sure you're not running guns?"

"Positive." Although she'd hoped to run into him, she was now irritated that he thought he could charm her again so easily. "Excuse me, Mr. Shaw. I was about to get some coffee for myself and my companion."

His mustache wiggled in a smile. "You have a good heart, don't you? Looking out for that old woman." He followed her to the table. "Could you leave her long enough to take a little walk outside with me? I need to stretch my legs before I get back on that train."

"I don't think so. Mrs. Gordon is a little nervous about being alone in the station."

He squinted over his shoulder. "Is that so?" He moved away from Heather. "I'll be right back."

Before she could say anything, he'd crossed the room on his long, long legs to take the seat next to Mrs. Gordon. The elderly woman smiled and waved her hand in a gesture of dismissal. Heather rolled her eyes and picked up the coffee. Ben had already started back toward her. Taking the cups from her hand, he led the way back to Mrs. Gordon.

"Thank you, Mr. Shaw," Mrs. Gordon said with a flirtatious inclination of her head. "Heather, honey, you go on. I'll just read my book."

Heather met Ben's laughing eyes with a sigh. A smile quirked the corners of her own mouth. "You win."

"I always win." He took her arm lightly and propelled her out the front door, carrying her coffee.

The night was crisp and cold, with a hint of snow in the air. Heather breathed deeply.

"Pretty night," Ben remarked, handing her the coffee. He led them to a wall and released her arm to survey the scene around them. Across the street, a huge hotel rose in glass and yellow light. Once, when Heather had made the layover in the morning, she had gone there for breakfast.

"Do you know the city?" she asked Ben.

"Not really. I was part of a seminar here one time, and I pass through a lot on the train, but I've never explored it. You?"

"No. What kind of seminar?"

"You mean you've never heard of me?" A teasing light touched his eyes, and Heather couldn't be sure if he was serious or not. His name did sound a little familiar, but she couldn't place just why.

"Should I have?"

"Probably not." He drew a cigarette out of his jacket pocket and lit it. Heather noted that his hands no longer trembled. "You don't seem the type to read Western novels."

"You're a writer?"

He nodded, then wiggled his nose and drew on the cigarette thoughtfully. "I'm told they're some of the most violent in the business."

"Well, then I probably wouldn't like them." She sipped the hot coffee. "It's interesting that you write, though. How did you get into that?"

He shrugged. "When I got out of the army, I needed something to do. I can't do some of the things I used to and my folks' ranch didn't need me. One day I was out on the range and I just started thinking about this story." He grinned. "It must've turned out okay, since I've been doing it ever since."

"I thought all writers had to struggle."

"Some do, some don't—just like anything else. I got lucky."

Heather looked at him. In the low light, his face was shadowed by the brushed hat. "So you were teaching writing at a seminar?"

"Yep. It was a lot of fun." He grinned at her. "Everybody thinks you're terrific."

"Are you?" The words sounded more flirtatious than she'd intended, but once uttered, she didn't know how to draw them back.

His smile crinkled the corners of his dark eyes and he leaned closer. His voice, as rich and deep as those eyes, held a playful note. "Depends on what you mean. I'm okay as a writer. I'm a good cook, too." He lifted a shoulder. "I'm not so terrific at heavy-equipment operation, though."

Her gaze flickered of its own accord to the plump lower lip beneath his mustache, and for one brief second, she allowed herself to wonder what it would be like to kiss him. In the next second, she straightened and asked, "Can you drive a car?"

"No."

Heather nodded. "I don't like driving. It always feels like there's too much going on. The train is nice and easy."

"How come you don't take a plane like everybody else?"

"The same reason I don't like cars. Besides, planes leave me breathless. You?"

"You leave me breathless."

Heather tsked. "Stop teasing," she said briskly. "Why don't you take planes?"

He tossed away his cigarette and leaned one elbow on the chest-high wall. "Bad memories." His tone was short. "Nothing to worry about."

"Do you have an echo chamber, too?"

"An echo chamber?" he repeated, musing. "Yeah. That's a good word for it." His arm touched hers as he leaned a little closer. "Did your husband have problems with flashbacks?"

She'd opened the conversation, Heather reminded herself. Although she ordinarily tried not to speak of James, here in the crisp dark of a strange city with a strange man, it seemed easier. "Yes. Sometimes very difficult problems."

"Not many people do, you know."

"I know." She smiled at him with a wistful glance. "But if you tell me you don't, I'll call you a liar."

"And you'd be right to. But it's not something I spend a whole lot of time worrying about." He touched his nose with one finger, like Santa Claus. "I figure life's too short to worry. You only get a certain number of days, and it's crazy to waste even one if you can help it.''

Heather cocked her head, looking at him with puzzlement.

As if he felt her gaze, he turned. His dark eyes glittered with humor. ''And that's why I'm out here with the prettiest woman I've seen in a long time. You can hide your hair, but you can't hide those eyes.''

A little portion of her shrunken soul relaxed under the caress of his warm voice, eased by the blunted syllables of his words. It was such an unfamiliar sensation that an accompanying fear bloomed, as well. She was suddenly deeply aware of his arm against hers, and shifted away from him.

He grinned, as if he knew why she'd moved. When he spoke, his voice wafted toward her as gentle and soft as a plume of smoke. ''A man could drown in your eyes, Heather.''

She knew she ought to, but she couldn't look away. For a long moment, she kept her eyes lingering on his, noting their weathered frame of sun lines and the long sweep of lashes that made their expression seem so gentle.

He straightened first, and Heather felt a small twinge of disappointment. ''I think it's probably time to get back inside,'' he said. ''Our train will be here soon.''

''Ours?'' she asked. ''Where are you headed, anyway?''

He smiled. "I'm a native of Pueblo. Didn't I tell you?"

Heather shrugged and shook her head, then followed him inside, trying to pretend it didn't matter that he lived close to her.

Ben didn't wander away as she'd expected, but stayed to chat with Mrs. Gordon and herself. When the train was announced, he walked with them to the platform. He took Mrs. Gordon's ticket from her hand and helped her find the right compartment. "Thank you, Mr. Shaw," she said coquettishly, and Heather smiled to herself. As they were about to walk away, the old woman grabbed Heather's arm. "Follow this one up, honey. I know a good man when I see one."

"I just met him on the train," Heather whispered.

"Meetings aren't as important as what comes after," she replied, and winked broadly. "I'll be your chaperon tomorrow if it makes you feel better."

Heather frowned and nodded distractedly. No doubt about it, this trip was becoming a little strange. She often shared the journey with a passenger who also had a long way to travel, but never had she felt, as she did with Mrs. Gordon and Ben, to be a part of a group, having something more in common than a train ride.

Ben waited at the end of the car. "Can I see you home?" he asked, holding out his arm.

"I'm sure I can find my way."

"I wasn't doubting your competence—just trying to be a gentleman." Again his eyes seemed to glitter with suppressed mirth, and Heather felt chastened. When had she learned to behave like a stuffy matron?

"Thank you, Mr. Shaw," she said with exaggerated good manners, and took his arm. "I should be very glad of your company."

It was, of course, impossible to maintain contact in the narrow hallways of the railway cars, and they often had to shimmy against the carpeted walls as a traveler passed with burdens of suitcases and shoulder bags. But each time a little space opened, Ben took her hand and again placed it over his elbow. His jacket was made of soft wool and Heather could feel the tendons of his arm move rhythmically below the fabric. He walked a little ahead of her and air currents carried the leathery scent of him to her nose. He was the kind of man, Heather thought, that would be good to hug. His embrace might carry hints of hunger, but he would also know how to hold a woman with ease and comfort.

He stopped at one of the larger rooms meant for families. "This one's mine," he said. "Just in case you want to find me tomorrow."

"Thank you," she responded dryly. "That's comforting."

"I knew you'd feel that way." He grinned and took her arm again, leading the way down the hall, past a staircase that led to more compartments and the rest rooms, into a very narrow hallway. He stopped about halfway down. "This is yours."

"Thank you." She slipped her guitar inside the door and faced him. "I think I can handle it from here."

He lifted her hand to his lips. His eyes lingered on her face with a hint of humor mixed with something else—admiration or appreciation—a very gentle something, anyway. His mouth brushed the bony back of her hand, his mustache prickling her skin deliciously. "It's been a pleasure to share your company, Heather," he said, not yet releasing her hand. "Will you let me buy you breakfast?"

She hesitated. What point was there, really? she wondered. Why spend so much time with someone she would probably never see again?

With a touch as light as a warm rain, he lifted his hand and trailed one finger down her cheek. It lingered at the corner of her mouth and landed on her chin. "Please? I'll invite Mrs. Gordon, too."

Heather laughed. She couldn't help it. "Okay."

"Then I'll say good-night."

"Goodnight," she replied firmly and dipped into her tiny cubicle. From the hallway, she heard his slightly uneven departure and wondered why she'd agreed to breakfast with him. Then she laughed at herself.

It wasn't terribly difficult to figure out either the attraction or the desire to spend more time with him. It was safe. Since chances were good—even if he did live in Pueblo—that she would never see him again, there was little possibility of their being anything but friends. She could even bask a little in the delicious warmth of a man's attention and allow herself the almost forgotten luxury of being attracted to him in return.

When she returned home, he would be a pleasant memory she could fall back on in the rough weeks facing her as the anniversary of her husband's death approached and passed. Experience had taught her that they would be rough weeks indeed.

In his room, Ben shucked his coat and boots and sat down with the lights off to watch the scenery of the night pass by. A lingering impression of Heather stuck with him. How, he thought in exasperation, had he gotten so lucky and unlucky all at once?

It was the story of his life—like the mine that had left him alive and gotten him out of Vietnam six months early, yet had left him with a crooked brain, a limp and nightmares for the rest of his life.

He wasn't prone to fantasies—at least not the romantic type, he thought with a twist of his mouth. His fantasies tended to be ugly visions of what could be balanced against what was. It was that dark thread that permeated his books, books he wrote to keep the nightmares at bay. It worked and made him money. It was enough.

Enough for him, anyway. He wondered if it would be enough for Heather. If she read one of his books, would she run? For violence and Vietnam were things she didn't want to think about. He wondered what had gone wrong with that husband of hers. He had a hunch it wouldn't be easy to get around that ghost.

He lit a cigarette. His mind told him there was no way it would work between them and that he had no business sticking his nose into her pain or her life.

But his heart had been seized the moment she stepped onto the platform in St. Louis, canceling out the usual horrors his brain supplied at such moments with a delicate vision of medieval beauty and grace. That had never happened in the almost twenty years since his injuries had occurred. To Ben, Heather was nearly an omen, and one he wouldn't let slip away.

No matter what, he had to live each moment. As irrational as it was, he intended to make Heather a part of as many of his moments as he could.

Chapter Three

In the middle of Kansas in the middle of the night, the train ground to a halt. Heather didn't wake immediately, but not long after it had stopped she missed the rocking motion of the coach and the rumbling of the engines. She sat up and looked out the window. Huge, thick flakes of snow dropped from a pinkish sky. Against the horizon, a barn stood in silhouette against the pale night, but there was nothing else but empty stretches of land. Had the snow stopped them? she wondered.

She got up and slipped into a pair of jeans and socks. The long-sleeved T-shirt she'd worn to bed was warm enough and she propped herself against the wall to watch the snow. In the hallway, she heard murmurs of concern and excitement, and even a snatch of conversation as passengers questioned the source of the delay.

After a little while, Heather turned on the lamp and pulled out her guitar. She had thought she might play earlier, but she'd been too tired. Now she felt wide-awake and music whispered along her nerves, urging expression. She tuned the instrument automatically, adjusting the nylon strings that set it apart from a regular guitar.

Slowly she began to play a quiet melody that had been born in one of her dreams one night. The tripping notes reminded her of water, of a cold mountain stream, of skipping stones in a huge lake, of rain on the mighty Mississippi—that river of her childhood. The music soothed Heather. She didn't even wonder what created the delay. Lost in her playing, she drifted into worlds unrelated to the moment.

A soft tapping at her door brought her back to the middle of Kansas. "Who is it?" she called out.

"Ben. Are you awake?"

She pulled the curtains aside. He was leaning against the wall, lines of fatigue pulling down his mouth. The hat was gone, and he wore a thick corduroy shirt the color of sand, over jeans. The light color emphasized the rich darkness of his eyes and hair. Without his hat, his hair fell over his forehead in unruly waves. Heather was struck again by his undeniably masculine good looks—a face as rugged as Arizona mesas. She smiled and opened the door. "Hi. Come in."

He eased himself onto the opposite end of the bed—the only place to sit since the bed took up the entire room. On his feet was a pair of well-worn moccasins in pale leather, with beads intricately applied to the tops in the pattern of a cross. He made a small sound of pain as he sat down.

"Are you all right?" Heather asked.

"Yeah." Ben grimaced. "This damn weather gets to me. If it gets wet, I get stiff as sure as dawn means morning."

"An unmistakable sign of advancing age," she teased.

"It's getting worse the older I get." He grinned wryly. "Now, weren't you playing that thing?"

"Yes. Would you like to hear something?"

"Yeah. Whatever you want to play."

His weariness touched her. She began with Mozart, a complicated piece to play, but well worth the effort for its lightheartedness. Because of the warm-up she'd done before he'd come in, it wasn't difficult, and she felt her mouth curving into a smile as her fingers flew over the strings. At the end, she grinned at Ben. "Whew. It's been a while since I tried that one."

He'd listened with his eyes closed, and his voice was gravelly when he spoke. "That was pretty."

"Mozart." He didn't need conversation, she decided. Company, perhaps. Definitely music. She bent her head over the neck of the guitar. Several compositions came to mind, and she settled upon only those filled with hope—anything lilting, anything with joy.

One was a rousing, intricate Spanish dance, complete with thumps on the body of her guitar. She finished with a flourish and laughed. "I love that one. It makes me think of a hundred things—all of them vigorous."

Ben smiled. He looked better, Heather thought. The sparkle was back in his eyes, and a ripple of satisfaction touched her.

"Did you know you didn't brush your hair?" he asked, teasing.

Heather reached up to smooth the braids and felt the loose hair around her head. "Well, you can't expect polish at three o'clock in the morning." She laid the instrument down next to her and reached up to pull out the elastic bands in her hair. Her purse hung on a hook near the door and she fished a brush from it. "Do you know what happened out there?" she asked, loosening the braids with her fingers.

Ben watched her with appreciation. Heather tried to remain natural, but without the armor of her guitar to shield her, she grew aware of her bralessness beneath the thin T-shirt. As if her breasts realized it themselves, their nipples tautened. She glanced at Ben to see if he'd noticed, pulling her hair over her shoulders as an extra layer of clothing. He smiled wryly and his eyes met hers gently.

"There was an accident on the tracks. A truck turned over and spilled out some kind of junk all over the road. It's a mess."

"Was anyone hurt?"

"Don't think so. The truck just turned over. The driver was okay." He stretched out a hand. "Would you let me brush your hair?"

"Are you kidding?" She handed over the brush and turned around. "I *pay* people to brush my hair for me."

"Really?"

She looked over her shoulder at him. "Have you ever heard of a joke?"

He grinned. Heather turned around and Ben began to brush her hair with long, smooth strokes. "Did it take a long time to grow your hair?"

"Most of my life. I've trimmed it often, but it's never been drastically cut."

"Never?"

"No. I wasn't allowed to when I was a little girl, and as I got older, I couldn't face it."

"Isn't it hard to take care of?"

"Not at all. People ask me that all the time, but I think it would be harder to have to curl your hair and style it and put mousse on it every day than weaving in a few braids."

"Does it get in your way?"

Heather smiled as the brushing relaxed her. "No. I'm used to it."

"I guess you would be." She felt him lift the brush and let a hank of hair fall. "God, it's pretty." He gathered all of it into his hands and made a rope. Heather shifted to look at him. He twined the pale length around one forearm. Her breath caught in her throat at the strangely intimate gesture. He stroked the hair with his other hand, as if it were an animal he was admiring. His fingers were clean and long, with neat, oval nails. He moved them steadily, deliberately over the coil around his wrist and Heather simply watched, enthralled by his absorption. After a moment, he looked at her with his deep, soft eyes.

Heather glanced away, feeling vulnerable and exposed.

He dropped the "rope," as if sensing her mood. "How'd you like to go see the scene of the accident?"

"It's the middle of the night!"

He smiled. "So? I'll protect you."

Heather raised her eyebrows. "Who will protect you?"

"I reckon I could handle almost anything."

"Bears?"

"Even a grizzly." He grinned. "If there was such a thing in a prairie this flat."

"Okay." She might as well—it certainly beat sitting in her cubicle. "I'll meet you at the top of the stairs in five minutes."

He struggled to a standing position, and Heather didn't miss his wince as his feet took his weight. She watched him silently as he limped out on obviously stiff legs.

A few minutes later, bundled in her thick coat and boots suitable for the coldest Missouri winter day, she met Ben at the arranged spot. He wore his hat and a heavy down parka. His cowboy boots thumped on the floor. "You're such a tiny thing," he remarked.

"I'm five-five. That's not tiny."

"I'm seven inches taller than you. That's tiny."

Outside, the air was soft with gigantic snowflakes, and the ground was covered with a thick blanket of white. Heather tasted the fresh air with pleasure. "Isn't it beautiful?"

"If you like snow."

"Don't you?"

"Sure. I like all weather. Some people are rabid about snow, though."

They walked along the tracks in the snowy field next to the rails. "You play the guitar like an angel," Ben said.

"How does an angel play the guitar?"

"You know what I mean. How long have you been playing?"

"Since I was eight. A friend of my father's found the guitar in an abandoned car he'd towed in with his wrecker, and my father bought it for ten dollars. I loved it. My parents gave me lessons."

"Why don't you find yourself a place with a symphony or something?"

"Not much call for guitarists in that capacity. I do occasional guest appearances and things like that." Her feet made no sound at all in the soft snow. "I'm not really that good. I'm competent—no more."

Ben took her arm. "No. You're much better than that."

His tall, warm body felt comfortable close to her and she glanced up at him with a brief smile. "If you were a musician you would understand what I mean."

"I'm no musician," he conceded. "But I've struggled with that damned instrument for most of my natural life and I know how hard it is to play really good guitar."

A wash of light illuminated his nose and jaw. Heather simply looked at him. It was flattering, of course, for someone to think she had talent. And perhaps she did—a small one. She also knew, with a clearsightedness born of fruitless tryouts, that she wasn't as gifted as he would like to believe. After a moment, she said, "I do love playing. The theater group I work with is doing *Twelfth Night* this weekend and all next week. Whenever there's a performance, I'm guaranteed an audience for my own music. Although it's fun to just play, composing is my true love."

As she spoke, she realized she rarely shared that deep center of herself with anyone. What was it about Ben Shaw that made her talk and talk and talk whenever he appeared? She turned away from him to look toward the dark scene in front of them. Ahead, the lights of a police car flashed on a road that would intersect the tracks around the next turn. "Are you sure no one was hurt?" she asked.

"Positive. The steward said the guy just fell asleep. The truck wasn't even mangled much. It's just a mess due to the cargo."

"I always hate it when people mob accident scenes."

"Gory, isn't it?" He paused. "This is a little different, though. And anyway, it's not like we have a TV to watch."

Heather smiled. "True. Not that I have one, anyway."

"You don't have a television?"

She shook her head. "I never watched it when I was a child, and I guess I just never got around to picking it up."

"Didn't your husband watch it?"

"Endlessly. But I always got restless." She looked at him. "Are you one of those die-hard addicts who watch everything?"

"Nah. I watch movies, mostly."

"You seem like you'd be one of those guys that spend Sunday afternoons glued to the games."

"Well, you're wrong," he said, squeezing her arm playfully.

"What do you do on Sunday afternoons, then?"

He slipped his hand down her arm and into her pocket. His fingers were ice cold. "Do you mind?" he asked, after he'd taken her hand in his.

"No," she replied softly. How could she mind? He felt like a chinook wind, gentle and warm, on the frozen stretches of her spirit. She gingerly touched the long fingers in her pocket.

"On Sunday afternoons," he said, "I take walks with my dog. Or I visit friends, or write. Sometimes, I treat myself to a movie in town or clean the house."

He leaned into her easily. "What do you do on Sundays?"

"Nothing, usually." Heather laughed. "Sleep late and listen to music."

He nodded. "That seems nice."

They rounded the curve that led to the accident and stopped at the activity. At least five police cars flashed their lights into the snowy night and dozens of down-clad workers struggled with the spilled boxes. The truck was a semi. The cab lay at a right angle to the trailer and the back doors had been flung open on impact, scattering the contents over the snow. Ben knelt to pick up a small box at his feet. He glanced inside and laughed heartily.

"What is it?" Heather asked.

"Electronic parts—for a computer manufacturer." He laughed again.

"Why are you laughing? Won't that cost the company a fortune?"

"Any company that lost this much stock would lose a fortune. This one can afford it better than a lot of others could." He tossed the box nearer the workers. "It's going to take them hours to clean this up."

Ben felt a sudden rigidity in the fingers clasped within his own and looked at Heather's face. The blue and red lights flashed over her pale skin. Her nostrils flared and he saw her swallow, a strangely stricken expression tightening the skin around her eyes. He caressed her fingers. "Is that how your husband died? In a car?"

She flickered her eyelids down over her huge eyes. "No," she answered abruptly.

Ben gnawed his inner cheek for a brief second. "Why don't we go back and get some hot chocolate?" he suggested quietly. He had an urge to enfold her very gently in his arms, to hold her and sooth that pain, whatever it was. He resisted. Instead, he pulled his hand from her pocket and stretched his arm around her shoulders. "It's too cold to stand around out here."

She leaned against him for a fleeting moment. Ben sighed very softly. As they walked, he wondered if his limp threw her off, and he felt an unusual sense of self-consciousness about it. Get over it, buddy, he told himself. Some women did find him less attractive because of his imperfection, but not any who mattered. A woman compassionate enough to take the coffee from his trembling hands wouldn't judge him over a bumpy walk.

Still, he had no wish to make her uncomfortable, and he moved his hand back to her elbow. They returned to the train without speaking.

When she would have headed for the dining cars, he tugged gently at her elbow. "The steward will bring it to my room. It's quieter there," he said. The truth was, he needed to pull his damn boots off again; the cold walk had made his ankle ache.

She measured him for a moment, her great eyes almost navy blue in her oval face. A wisp of hair clung to an eyelash and he reached up to brush it away. "No funny business," he assured her. "I promise."

A little light gleamed in her eyes. "I don't know why I trust you," she commented. "But I do."

"Good." He pressed her arm and released her. A steward stood at the top of the steps and Ben paused. "Will you bring some hot chocolate to my room?"

"Yes, sir."

Ben frowned briefly. "Is there any way you could bring a pot, instead of those dinky little cups?"

The young man grinned. "Sure, Mr. Shaw."

His room was much larger than Heather's. It was situated in a corner of the car and boasted a bathroom of its own. The bed had been made up, along the wall, and a chair faced the snowy scene outside. "What luxury," Heather murmured.

"I may as well travel in comfort, since I have to do so much sometimes."

"Do you travel a lot?" she asked, sitting gingerly on the chair.

"It depends on my mood. I had to work out some business with my agent. I figured I could use the change of scenery, so decided to do it in person." He sank down on the bed and winced. It was a fleeting expression, but Heather caught it and felt a response rise in her chest, an emotion she didn't stop to analyze.

"You should rest," she urged. When he reached down to yank at his boot, she moved easily to his feet and grabbed the heel. "Pull."

The boot slipped free and Heather grabbed the other one. Ben eased that foot out more gently, groaning softly as he did so. "Thank you," he said.

Heather returned to her chair. "Sure. No one should have to take off their own boots."

He grinned. "Do you want some help with yours?"

"No, thank you." She shrugged out of her coat. "I'd like to stay dressed in the company of a gentleman."

His smile was appreciative as he removed his own coat and took off his socks. Again, there was the slightest pause as he struggled to reach his left foot, and when he had wrestled the sock off, Heather saw the crisscross of scar tissue along his ankle.

"I see why the weather aggravates you."

He shrugged. "Truthfully, everything aggravates this leg. But life doesn't end with a few aches and pains."

Heather nodded. For a brief moment, thoughts of James brushed her mind, and she resolutely ignored them. "It looks like someone worked pretty hard to put it back together for you."

"I sort of got the impression you didn't like hearing about this stuff." His brown eyes fastened on her soberly.

She sighed and glanced away, then back at him. "I'm sure you think I'm a little strange. I'm sorry if I gave you that impression."

"I don't think you're strange at all." He grinned crookedly. "Just a little gun-shy."

She liked his face, she thought—liked the radiating lines around his eyes and the deep tone of his irises; liked the soft look of his multihued mustache and the strength in his jaw and chin. It was a face that was easy to look at, a face that hinted at a complex and interesting nature. "Yes," she agreed softly. "Gun-shy is a good way of putting it."

His eyes tilted up in humor. "I can handle that." He slipped his moccasins on and tied them. "My left leg, to answer your question, was shattered. They spent a lot of hours in quite a few operations piecing it back together, but there wasn't any way to get it perfect. It's got about a dozen pins to hold it all together and it's always stiff." He patted his pocket for cigarettes. "But basically I figure I'm lucky to walk at all." He held up the pack. "Does smoke bother you?"

"Not a bit. I smoked for ten years."

"How long since you quit?"

"About four years." She swallowed in memory. She and James and planned to have a baby—a baby that had never materialized.

"That's great." He brushed his wavy dark hair off his forehead and exhaled. "I don't imagine I'll ever give it up."

A knock at the door signaled the arrival of their hot chocolate, and Heather jumped up. "You sit. I'll take care of it." At the door she paused in chagrin and turned to look at him apologetically. "I don't have my purse."

He laughed and reached into his pocket for a wad of loose bills. "Give him a five for a tip."

Heather raised her eyebrows but did as she was told, taking the tray with its fat pot from the young man and giving him the money and the five-dollar tip. She was rewarded with a broad grin.

"I'll bet they fight to get you in restaurants," she remarked, closing the door. She put the tray down on a small table and poured each of them a cup of the creamy hot chocolate.

"Have you ever done that kind of work?"

"Yes. Often."

"Then you know how hard it is to please folks."

"I'm certainly not criticizing. In fact," she said with a smile, "I'm impressed."

"Don't be. Money's meant to be shared."

Another man might have felt he'd earned the right to treat waiters and clerks with condescension. Not many people felt obligated to share their wealth. As he leaned forward to sip his chocolate, she looked at the lustrous darkness of his hair. What, she wondered, would that hair feel like under her fingers? She glanced down the slant of his cheekbone and dropped to the broad, lean frame of his shoulders beneath the sand-colored corduroy shirt. She was jolted by a long-forgotten ripple of sexual awareness in her belly as his soft gaze tangled with her wandering one. A dawning expression of comprehension touched his eyes and some emotion flared there for a second. Heather sipped her chocolate hurriedly and burned her lips, sending a sting of tears to her eyes; when she pulled the cup away, she nearly spilled it in her lap. "I don't know what's wrong with me," she said with irritation. "I'm not ordinarily this clumsy."

Ben shifted until he was close to her. His voice held a hint of laughter when he asked, "Are you saying I shake you up?"

At his nearness, Heather felt her nervousness accelerate and she laughed shakily, unable to look at him. The leathery scent of him penetrated her nostrils, and unconsciously she inhaled it. "I don't know. I mean, I—no."

He laughed and brushed her hair away from her face. For an instant, his hand lingered on her shoulder, then dropped away. "I'm putty in the hands of such a beautiful woman. You don't have to be afraid of me."

She looked into his eyes. His lips were only a few inches from her own and yet he simply held her searching gaze without making any move to kiss her. It was strangely intimate, almost more penetrating than his kiss would have been. After a moment, she straightened. "All right."

He stubbed out his cigarette. "Do you know how to play backgammon?"

"I love it," she answered eagerly. "Do you have a board with you?"

"Right here." Ben pulled a small leather case from a bag beside the bed and opened it. "Dark or light?" he asked, extracting two soft bags of playing pieces.

"It doesn't matter. Light."

He spread the mat on the bed. "Come on over here. I promise I won't bite." When she'd moved, he handed her the bag of clear crystal disks.

She poured them into a pile and spread them into a single layer on the dark blanket of the bed, taking pleasure in their glowing sheen. After a moment, she followed Ben's lead and put the pieces in place on the well-crafted board. "This is a beautiful set," she commented.

"One of my sisters gave it to me for Christmas a few years back." He held a handful of round red glass pieces in his palm and fiddled with them. "I warn you. I'm very good and I like to win. Not even a pretty woman gets mercy from me."

"Is that so? Well, Mr. Shaw, I assure you I won't need any mercy."

As they played, it became obvious the two were well matched. Heather started out strong with two naturals, rolls that allowed her to strengthen her home position, and Ben glanced at her with a quirk of his mustache. He worked within the handicap easily, but Heather countered. It was only when a roll forced her to leave a man open that Ben took the lead, getting his men off the board a full two rolls before Heather did.

She cut short his chortle of victory with a demand for a rematch.

They played for two hours, trading victory and defeat between them. When they agreed to quit, Ben was one game behind. "I'm not going to let you get away with this, you know. I can't stand to lose this game."

"Especially to a woman?" Heather prompted.

He frowned. "Woman *or* man," he corrected. "I know I use a lot of *darlin's* and *sugars* and *honeys* when I talk, but that's just the way I was raised."

"I'll give you a chance to make up your losses tomorrow, then."

"You mean later today."

She smiled in agreement. "I guess I do. What time is it, anyway?"

"Around six, I'd say. It's starting to get light."

"It's morning?" Heather said in surprise. "I'm not even tired."

"It's the invigorating companionship."

"Must be," she replied, smiling. Still, she stood. "I wonder how long it's going to take them to clean up?"

Ben stood, as well. "Could be a while yet. Tired or not, we both ought to get some rest. The halls are too noisy in the daytime."

"You're right."

"I'll walk you to your room."

She didn't demur this time. Heather noted that his limp seemed worse as they walked the short distance to her cubicle—a fact he seemed to be trying to hide. "That limp doesn't bother me, you know," she commented without looking at him. "Relax."

He glanced at her and laughed a little, and she heard the slightly unsettled surprise in the deep notes. "Habit," he answered briefly.

At her room they stopped. "Thank you for the game," Heather said, turning to look up at him.

Ben lifted one hand to her chin, cupping it with his long fingers. For a moment he simply held it, stroking the underside of her jaw easily, his gaze taking inventory of her face. After a moment, he smiled. "Thank you," he returned, "for a nice day all the way around."

His lips touched hers, warm and surprisingly full. His mustache met the bowed lines of her upper lip in delicate greeting, and his mouth took hers firmly. Heather tilted her head into the cradle of his fingers, unable to think of a reason why she shouldn't give in to her wish to relax with him.

The kiss was as gentle as the man himself—undemanding and giving, with a hint of delicious sensuality in the swell of his lower lip. Heather parted her lips and he teased between her teeth with his tongue, flicking the very inner edges of her lips and the tip of her tongue. The softly probing sensuality sent a sudden sharp shock of pleasure through her middle. For a moment she let herself drift in the forgotten pleasure of a man's touch; the primitive, delicious luxury of feeling small and protected as his shoulders shielded her from any danger—real or imagined. His callused palm was cool along her jaw and the bushy mustache held the scent of his after-shave.

It was over far too quickly for Heather, and she pulled back a shade reluctantly when he released her, sliding his hand down her arm to take her hand, where he pressed another kiss to her palm. He sighed very quietly.

"You make me feel good, Heather, in ways I can't even tell you." He touched the pad of her thumb with his own. "I'd like to take you in there and do a lot more than kiss you, but I've got a hunch a one-night stand isn't your style."

At this reminder of the transient nature of their meeting, Heather felt a wisp of regret. "You're right," she confirmed. "I've probably let too much happen already."

He smiled. "No morals committee is going to call you up on charges of a few games of backgammon and a good-night kiss." He kissed her forehead—his lips moist against her skin—and released her. "See you later, Heather. Sleep well."

"Good night, Ben."

She entered her cubicle to find the morning sun weakly pushing at the heavy clouds. The light was eerie, with the falling snow casting a pink light, and the obscured sun was a pale yellowish globe, huge on the Eastern horizon. At its edges, the clouds shimmered in the palest shade of lavender.

Heather sank to her knees, transfixed by the incredible scene, then picked up her guitar in inspiration to play the music that suddenly burst into being in her mind. The notes carried foreign overtones, inspired by the unusual dawn, and she found her fingers picking out a double melody in a minor key that made her think of dancers from the Dark Ages, swirling in pagan and sultry invitation. In a fever of creativity, she rustled through her purse to find something to write on, hurriedly sketching out bars in the margins of a church program, capturing enough of the tune that she could play it again later.

When the sun rose a little higher, the heavy clouds dimmed the pastel lighting to a monochromatic gray. Heather put aside her guitar with a sigh of artistic satisfaction, and without even removing her shoes, pulled the blanket over her head and slept. Her last conscious thought was a half-realized wish that Ben had lingered long enough to view that alien beauty with her. Something told her he would have understood her rush to capture the song of the eerie dawn.

Chapter Four

When Heather awoke, the familiar thrum and rattle of the train told her the wreck had been cleaned up. Outside, a watery sun filtered through a light haze of clouds. She sat up groggily, stiff from not moving for several hours, and blinked at the snow-covered prairie over which the train traveled.

Her hand fell on the church program she'd used to record the dawn-inspired composition. She yawned broadly as she glanced over it, a sense of pleasure spreading through her chest as she remembered the lilting, exotic tone of the notes. Good, she thought; a new composition. There hadn't been a new one in almost a year—not unless she counted the ongoing work on the steel-mill piece, which had been in progress for some time.

She stood up and stretched, suddenly conscious of deep hunger. It was hard to remember the last thing she'd had to eat—oh, yes, the hamburger with Mrs. Gordon.

As she changed her clothes and made preparations for a trek to the bathroom downstairs, she let her mind touch briefly upon Ben. Had he already eaten? They'd made plans for breakfast before the accident—perhaps they no longer stood. The thought gave her a vague sense of disappointment.

The bathroom mirror showed her hair to be thoroughly disheveled, and Heather was momentarily embarrassed that she'd ventured out of her room in such a condition. Her usual habit was to braid it at night in order to save the tedious combing-out in the morning. Last night Ben had brushed it for her, then she'd left it down as an insulator against the cold. When she'd returned to her compartment, the sunrise had so stirred her creative juices that she'd never given her hair another thought.

She sat down on the toilet seat in the tiny bathroom and began to gingerly pull the tangles free, starting at the bottom and working her way up in an automatic gesture born of years and years of fighting the rat's nest of fine hair. As her fingers found and worked through some of the larger knots, she gradually became aware of a new sensation, one of tingly awareness and energy—even anticipation. What would the day bring? She hummed a part of the Mozart guitar piece she'd played for Ben the night before.

Suddenly the notes died in her throat as she pinpointed the emotion: infatuation. How ridiculous. She'd met a stranger on a train who teased her and made her feel attractive—and the next day she was singing. Boy, she thought in disgust, so much for the grieving widow.

And for what? For a man she would never see again? A man who had the same kind of history as her dead husband, and a past she obviously didn't have the tools to handle?

Having smoothed out the tangles in her hair, she stood up to wash her face. The cold water brought some color into her pale skin. Examining that face in the ugly fluorescent light, she thought it might be time for a makeup overhaul. Perhaps a trip to a cosmetics consultant at one of the department stores could help her choose shades that would emphasize her eyes and hide the lack of definition and color in the rest of her face.

Again she heard her thoughts with a touch of disbelief. As a teenager, she had, like most girls, experimented with dozens of shades of eye shadow and eyeliner and lipstick and foundation. Most of it looked ghastly on her, and Heather settled for a simple routine that hid the worst of her faults—a tendency to dark circles under her eyes, and the extreme paleness of her ivory skin.

But who would she be trying all this new makeup for? Her fish? The parakeets, maybe? The thought made her laugh, and she left the bathroom in search of food.

In the sparsely populated dining car, Heather ordered a big breakfast of French toast, orange juice and tea. When the waiter brought her tea, she asked, "Where are we?"

"Kansas. We'll get to the next station in about an hour."

"Do you know when we'll get to La Junta?"

"We're running almost exactly four hours behind, ma'am."

Heather stifled a smile over the "ma'am" and nodded. "Thank you."

She wondered where Ben was as she ate her elegant breakfast, served with as much of an aura of a posh hotel as the train company could muster. Surely he wasn't still sleeping at noon—but perhaps he was, she argued. Maybe he wasn't a morning person. Maybe he was working—his was the sort of profession, like music, that could be pursued on a train, after all. Or maybe he'd found more interesting companionship.

It irritated her that so many of her thoughts centered around the enigmatic writer; yet she couldn't deny the pulsing energy that enlivened her this morning.

After she'd eaten, she wandered back through the train to her room, feeling a little lonely. She'd stopped by Mrs. Gordon's cubicle to find the old woman already gone, and there was nothing left to do except return to her own little space. Once there, determined not to read more into the previous evening's activities than there had actually been, she straightened the tiny room and made the bed into seats again, then sat down with her guitar and the church program.

She was soon deeply engrossed in her music, as her restless energy found relief in the unusual composition. She wandered through what she remembered a few times, then set about refining and magnifying the piece. After digging out a notebook from her canvas carry-all, she carefully penciled in regular rows of musical bars where she recorded what she discovered. She played a few notes, hummed them back to herself with variations, played the variations, and recorded in musical notation what she heard.

When a knock interrupted her, Heather's heart slammed into her rib cage. She paused for a moment, embarrassed by her physical reaction. Ben's voice floated through the door: "Heather?"

Of course. He'd heard her playing. Now he must be wondering why she wasn't answering. An acute sensation of panicky anticipation clutched her stomach for a moment—and then she laughed at herself. How old are you, anyway? she asked herself wryly before opening the door.

He wore the same cream-colored corduroy shirt as he had the day before. His eyes glinted merrily, and the smallest hint of a smile clung to his mouth. Before

Heather could move, that mouth swept down and brushed her own in greeting. "Mornin'," he said.

"It's not really morning, you know," she corrected. Beneath the prim words, her heartbeat skidded into a more normal pattern, but Ben's body seemed to fill the doorway and his scent surrounded her with a pervasive, powerful masculinity. Her gaze fell to his chest.

"It's morning for me. Have you eaten?"

Heather nodded. An almost unnaturally glistening curl of hair had snaked under his collar. She barely resisted lifting her fingers to reposition it with its brothers.

"You want to come with me while I get something? I'd sure enjoy the company."

"I'd like that." She raised her eyes to meet his.

Ben didn't move, but a sudden flare of heat warned her he wouldn't be content to play patient forever. She met that gaze, too, thinking now with her soul—with that portion of herself from which her music sprang— and wondered what melody would come when she was wrapped in his lean, hard arms. He moved first, taking his arm from the doorway where he'd braced himself, and glanced down the hallway. "We can get the backgammon board on the way, and you can let me make up my losses," he said, giving her room to retreat.

"*Let* you? Ha!"

"We'll see." He stopped at his compartment for the board and they continued their walk. "What were you playing in there when I interrupted?"

"Something new. I don't know what it is yet." She pressed against the wall to let someone pass. "Did you see the sunrise this morning?"

"No, I didn't. Was it nice?"

"Oh, Ben, it was beautiful." She touched his arm instinctively. "I can't tell you how beautiful."

"Try." He took her hand. "But save it for a minute so I can hear you properly."

They maneuvered the rest of the corridors to the dining car in silence. "Would you like a cup of coffee or something?"

"A cup of tea would be nice, thank you."

He ordered for both of them, then turned his attention fully to Heather and, lighting a cigarette, said, "Now tell me about this sunrise."

Heather let the scene fill her mind for a minute before she spoke. "It was like something from another planet. The sun was huge and soft, and the sky turned violet all around the edges—" She broke off, suddenly aware that the words somehow didn't express what she had seen. "I'll have to play my new composition for you. It says what I can't."

"I'd like that." He sipped his heavily sugared coffee with relish. "Mmm. That tastes good. I got some new ideas last night—or rather, this morning—too."

"Can you share them? Or are you one of those writers who can't talk about what you're doing?"

He wiggled his nose above the mustache. "Generally I can. These feel so different, I think I'm afraid to say them out loud. Maybe they'll disappear." He touched her hand. "I'll tell you that you inspired them, though."

Her ears tingled, but thankfully the waiter arrived with Ben's breakfast—a warmed sweet roll drenched in melting butter, with bacon, eggs, grits and biscuits. Heather's eyes widened. When the waiter also placed a pitcher of a clear red liquid alongside, she shook her head. "Is that Kool-Aid?"

Ben grinned broadly, his eyes dancing. "My terrible secret addiction."

She laughed. "I can't believe anyone still eats like this. Don't you know all that cholesterol and fat will kill you?"

"Something's going to do it eventually," he said, picking up his fork. "My grandpa ate like this all of his life and he lived until he was eighty-three."

Ben ate with relish and Heather watched in fascination, conscious of the tingling awareness she'd noticed that morning spreading and growing through her body. He was lean and handsome and charming and kind. Why in the world should she resist him? How long had it been since she'd felt so alive? If it ended the moment the train pulled in, so be it. At least she would have had a few healing hours in the company of a man who made her feel like a woman.

Mrs. Gordon stopped at their table, with a man close to her age in tow. "Hello, you two. I guess I'm the only one on the train to have slept through the accident, except my acquaintance Harry, here. We were the only ones moving when the kitchen opened this morning.''

The elderly gentleman, portly and with thinning silver hair, smiled in greeting. ''Neither of us ever knew what had happened.''

''Would you like to join us?'' Ben asked.

''Oh, no, thank you, honey,'' Mrs. Gordon replied. ''We're on our way to the observation car. I just wanted to stop and say hello.'' She reached out and squeezed Heather's arm, giving her a hidden wink.

Heather grinned. After the older woman had departed, she said, ''Mrs. Gordon thinks you're quite a catch.''

Ben raised one dark eyebrow and a lock of hair fell on his forehead. The combination gave him a rakish look. ''I am,'' he replied.

''No man is a good catch if a woman isn't fishing,'' Heather countered.

He smiled in appreciation. ''True.'' He stacked his dishes to one side, took a large sip of the jewel-colored Kool-Aid and dabbed at his lip with the heavy linen napkin. ''Much better. Are you ready for that rematch?''

''Are we allowed to play here?''

''I don't see why not.''

''Okay.'' She shifted her tea to one side. ''Prepare to lose, Mr. Shaw.''

Again, as on the night before, the competition was rich with laughter and concentration. They played for a long time, keeping score on a scrap of paper the waiter produced. The train slipped from Kansas into Colorado, and the afternoon shadows lengthened. When Heather happened to glance up and see the bluish line of the Rocky Mountains on the horizon, a finger of regret touched her belly. Almost home. The thought should have given her relief, but the emotions she felt were quite the opposite. Her preoccupation caused her to overlook a trap Ben had set for her, and he laughed good-naturedly as he knocked one of her counters off the board. "Had enough?"

Heather nodded wryly. "We're almost there, anyway."

He nodded. "'Bout that time, I guess."

"I think I'm going to go get my things together."

"I'll walk you back."

"That would be nice." She slipped the glass playing pieces back into their soft bags. There was a sudden uncomfortable awkwardness between them. What now? Heather wondered.

His eyes met hers as she handed him the bags, and Heather knew there was laughter lurking deep in those unfathomable irises now. "What are you laughing about?"

"Am I laughing?"

"Not on the outside."

"Do you read minds?"

Heather rolled her eyes and smiled. "No. I read eyes. And if eyes ever danced, yours are dancing now."

At this, he broke into a full-fledged grin, and Heather noticed again how naturally the lines of his face arranged themselves for smiling, as if it had been formed to break into easy laughter over and over and over. "I think," he said quietly, "that you may have gotten to like me a little, Titania."

She blushed and looked away. How could she answer? She nodded imperceptibly.

He walked her to her roomette and left her there with a gentle squeeze of her arm. "See you, Heather. Thanks for the backgammon."

A thousand words crowded into her mouth and she uttered none of them. There was no point. If she had let herself become infatuated with a stranger on a train, she deserved to feel the hurt that was now creeping in. "Goodbye, Ben," she whispered as she let herself into her compartment.

At the sight of the neat bars of her new composition resting on the small table, she sighed. She'd wanted to play it for him. Too bad she wouldn't have the chance.

By the time the train reached the La Junta station, darkness had fallen and a deep cold frosted the air. Heather grabbed up her belongings and bundled up, ready for the long drive to Pueblo. She didn't much like the trip in the dark, for the roads were narrow country highways with no streetlights and lots of open fields. There was no help for it. She was going to miss the rehearsal tonight, as well. But there was no help for that, either. By now, everyone would be gathered at the theater. She would call Mike when she got home and apologize. It wasn't as if she didn't know her music; it was an original composition she'd written several years before that had fit the theme of the play.

When the train stopped, she was waiting at the door to disembark, and within minutes she had her guitar nestled in the back seat of her car and her bag in the trunk.

Ben cursed himself when he found her cubicle empty. He'd been teasing Heather a little, letting her think they would now part company, hoping perhaps, in some way, to jolt her a little. Now it seemed like a childish trick, and he was ashamed of himself.

The truth was, she unsettled him. All that delicacy of language and bearing was, for a man of his ranching and rodeo background, a little out of left field. It served him right if she got away before he'd had a chance to properly say goodbye.

He hurried through the corridors and out into the dark cold of the La Junta station. He caught a flash of pale gold hair in the gleam of a streetlight and ran for the parking lot. "Heather!"

She turned in confusion. When, over the black top of her car, she saw Ben hobbling toward her, there was relief and hope on her face. Good, he thought. He wasn't wrong—she *did* like him a little. Breathlessly he paused next to her.

For a very long moment, neither of them said a word. Ben was winded and Heather simply didn't speak as she looked up at him with those huge eyes. A quiver of longing rippled in his loins, a sensation he quelled immediately. He reached out to touch her hair, which glimmered in the soft light, and slid his palm from the crown of her head to her shoulder. "I enjoyed this train ride more than anything I've done in years, Heather. Thank you." His hand moved below the curtain of hair to the tender flesh of her warm neck and circled it.

Heather caught her breath. All of the alert awareness she'd noticed during the last few hours bloomed in her skin where his hand touched her. His gentle gaze washed over her face, as if memorizing every line. Heather couldn't breathe. Everything within her strained toward him, and she swayed into his waiting embrace.

He dropped his other hand to her waist and pulled her against him. For the first time Heather felt his full, lean length pressed into her, felt the surprising hardness of his thighs and arms below cushioning layers of clothing. Her hands reached up in a half-remembered gesture of defense and landed upon his chest, where her fingers splayed of their own accord. His leathery, smoky aroma enveloped her and she lifted her eyes to meet his gaze.

"You are so beautiful," he whispered, brushing his hand reverently over her face and hair.

Strong hands, Heather thought, as his thumb brushed her earlobe.

He brought his mouth to hers with infinite care. The gentleness was so unthreatening, so sweet, that Heather felt herself responding without fear, lulled by his easy embrace and tender caresses. She relaxed into him, gingerly kissing him back with an emotion of gratitude, an emotion that melted away to nothing as the playful sensuality she'd sensed in his kiss this morning rose to the forefront. He slid and teased his lips over hers—Heather could almost feel his smile.

He tightened his arms about her and she arched to meet him with a surge of longing completely new to her. Sensing her shift in attitude, Ben parted her lips with his tongue as gently as the morning sun slips over the horizon, and Heather responded like a morning glory, opening the blossoms of her lips to his luxurious warmth. She tilted her head to reach him more fully and he brushed the tip of his cold nose against her cheek as she fit her mouth more securely into the frame of his. Unconsciously, she moved her fingers over his chest and into the deep silk of his cold, heavy hair. The flesh of his neck and scalp were warm and she combed through that weight of hair with languorous delight. She gave a small sigh.

Ben lifted his head slightly to smile at her. No panic or shyness touched her. She smiled back and he tickled her cheek with his mustache. "It's been real nice,

Heather." He swallowed and the corded muscle of his jaw flexed. "I hate to let you go."

So he didn't. He wrapped her tightly in an engulfing, warming hug, pressing their bodies together with fierce care. Heather nestled her face perfectly into the hollow of his shoulder and his jacket scratched her cheek. He held her a long time, rocking slightly, and Heather closed her eyes. There was no eroticism in the hug—just tenderness; a heartbreaking reverence. She clung to him, wrapping her arms around his shoulders and neck, breathing in deeply the good, outdoorsy smell of his skin. She wanted to go on forever, holding him in the cloudy darkness; but when his arms loosened, she reluctantly relaxed her hold, as well.

He kissed her again quickly. "Maybe I'll see you in Pueblo," he said, and released her. "You drive carefully."

Heather nodded, her throat tight. A strange prickling of tears gathered behind her eyes and she blinked hard and swallowed to chase them away. "Take care, Ben," she managed, and drew her hand away from his. "It was very nice to meet you."

He gave her a halfhearted grin and touched her cheek. "Bye."

Just like that, he walked away—a tall, lean man in jeans and corduroy jacket, his thick dark hair catching bits of light as he passed under the streetlamps. Heather sighed and got into the car. "Journeys end in lovers parting," she quipped aloud to herself; it made her feel better to slaughter Shakespeare. And she started the car.

All the way home, her heart ached.

Chapter Five

When Heather awoke the next morning in the familiar surroundings of her bedroom, the whole trip home from St. Louis seemed like a dream—impossible to imagine.

Last night, she'd barely dropped her bags by the door and made it to the shower before tumbling into bed. After the interrupted night of sleep on the train and the long journey, her body had needed the rest, however invigorated she'd felt. She'd slept a solid twelve hours, she noted as she washed her face in the big bathroom of her 1930s-era house. Sunlight streamed through the glass brick of the room, lighting the maroon tiles with their slender lines of pink and the cross-stitch of a castle on a hill Heather's mother had made for her a birthday or two before. She kept thinking the room could use a plant or two, but with typical forgetfulness, she'd never gotten around to buying one, or even moving one in from another room.

She wandered into the kitchen in her bathrobe and put on a pot of water for tea. Coffee would do in a pinch, while traveling or on a break during a show, but Heather much preferred tea, and she boasted a large collection of various exotic blends from all over the world. No herbal teas, either. She preferred full-bodied teas with musky scents and hearty flavor, without sugar or milk to dilute it. This morning she chose a Formosan blend she'd found in a shop in nearby Colorado Springs, and while she waited for the water to boil, picked up a tray of various boxes of food from the counter to feed her pets.

Her parakeets and fish had been cared for by a neighbor in her absence, but at the first sounds of the Handel suite Heather chose to play on her impressive stereo, the birds set up a racket and she laughed as she fed them. "Did you miss me, gentlemen?"

Amadeus chirped and quirked his head appealingly. Heather opened the cage and let the blue-and-white bird perch on her finger while she stroked his feathered head. Peter, a cream-colored parakeet with the faintest tinge of yellow, skittered over to the farthest bar from the door of their enclosure. "Going to punish me, Peter?" He blinked and turned his head away. Heather lifted Amadeus to the roof of his cage and attended to her fish—a school of neon tetras and half a dozen angelfish housed in an octagonal sixty-gallon tank. The birds and fish had been the only expenditures she'd made with the rather large inheritance from James's grandfather that had passed to her upon James's death—money she hadn't wanted and still refused to use except for house payments. Only a modest sum was kept in her savings account. The rest—more money than her father had made in his lifetime—had been reinvested at the advice of her banker.

It had only been upon the urging of James's brother Mike that Heather had bought the birds and fish as a tonic for her loneliness. She'd never been able to rationalize using money that should have been James's, except to pay for the house that he'd worked so hard to restore. Although it wasn't the kind of house she would have picked for herself, it did seem to embody everything about Pueblo that she loved. The preponderance of glass brick bespoke the fondness the Slavs who had settled this part of town with their earnings from the steel mill had had for grace and neatness. The large, square rooms with their arches and plastered walls told of the craftsmanship those sturdy people had demanded. And in the backyard, the carefully manicured lawn with its tulips, irises, rosebushes and chrysanthemums assured color all summer long. Even the large, untrimmed catalpa trees that cast protective shadows through the heat of the summer days spoke to Heather of foresight and planning. This house, she knew, had been built to be lived in for a lifetime.

The teakettle whistled sharply and she returned to the kitchen for her tea. Through the windows, on the eastern horizon, the black, now smokeless stacks of the steel mill stood against the sky—an endlessly fascinating view.

As she waited for her tea to brew, the phone rang. Heather grabbed it up—irrationally, briefly hoping to hear Ben's voice. As soon as she heard her heart speaking, she rolled her eyes at herself and her gruff "Hello" reflected her irritation with herself.

"Where the hell have you been, Heather? I've been worried sick." It was Mike, James's brother and director of the play.

"Oh, Mike, I meant to call you last night when I got in, but it was late and I was so tired, I forgot."

"What happened?"

"The train was delayed in Kansas in the middle of the night and we were four hours behind, getting in. Even by the time I got to La Junta, I knew I wouldn't have been able to catch you." She stirred her tea. "How did the rehearsal go?"

"Good. You can make it tonight, can't you?"

"Sure. I think I'm supposed to go in for a fitting this morning, too."

"I'll probably see you there, then. I have a lot to do."

"Do you want to have some lunch at Nick's or something?"

"You buying?"

Heather laughed. "Of course I am, if I'm eating with you."

"Good girl. I'll see you at the theater in a couple of hours, then."

Before her fitting, she had a class to teach—a class offered through the adult-education program the city organized. Like most of her jobs, it didn't pay much— all of them altogether barely paid her enough to keep the wolves from the door; thus her forced reliance on some portion of James's inheritance—but the internal rewards were high. Most of her students in this six-week term had been with her for the past three sessions, and two of them were beginning to show a great deal of progress. She knew that for those two students, this weekly class was one of their high points. She found it gratifying to contribute her skills as a teacher. As she'd pointed out to Ben, her talent wasn't large enough to permit her to make recordings of her compositions or to achieve the kind of success some other guitarists had, but the small jobs she did added up to a satisfying life, anyway. She taught and composed and provided music for the theater group—even occasionally was asked to do recitals.

She dressed in a red challis skirt and a flowing blouse, pulled on her boots and wove her hair into one long braid. From the dozens of ribbons on a hanger in the bathroom, she chose a very long one of red velvet and wrapped it around the braid in medieval fashion.

Although the sun was shining, the morning was a cold one and Heather's aging economy car was stubborn about starting. She pumped the gas pedal and shook the ignition key several times to coax the first cough from the engine, and it took several more tries before the motor caught—only to die once more. Heather sighed and let the battery rest a moment. She would have to buy a new car before much longer. It wasn't just the starting on cold mornings; the car needed an engine overhaul and it was only a matter of time before it had to be done. The work would cost more than buying a reasonably priced used car, and although she was sentimental about some things, her car wasn't one of them. Cars, she thought as she grimly turned the key once more, were nothing more than a necessary evil. How people ever had love affairs with such cantankerous, mean-spirited, baffling machines was beyond her.

The morning went well. Her class was eager and cheerful, and one of her favorite students had been practicing a fairly difficult piece at home, which he played for Heather's approval. The other students, far from being envious, were enthusiastic and supportive. After class, Heather took him aside and urged him to seek more extensive training. "I think you have a lot of natural ability. There are some excellent instructors at the university. You should think about getting enrolled."

Tom was close to Heather in age, and had unruly dark hair, a long, narrow face and full lips. He gave her a wry smile. "I didn't finish high school."

"So get your general equivalency diploma, Tom. You're bright, you've had enough experience to be able to handle university now."

He didn't look as if he believed her. "It's a nice idea," he said. "I'll give it some thought."

Heather backed off with a smile. "Do that. You really *are* talented. It would be a shame to waste that."

Another wistful smile touched his face and he wandered off. For a moment, Heather wondered why he was reluctant. Then she realized the time and hurried off to the fitting.

Her class and the play were both housed in the Sangre de Cristo Arts Center. The sprawling complex in downtown Pueblo boasted a fine theater, an art gallery of some renown, and a series of smaller rooms designed for instruction in ballet and all manner of classes for adults and children in a wide array of subjects ranging from lessons in beadwork to painting to Southwestern history. Heather dashed to the fitting rooms in the bowels of the theater and found Mike in deep conversation with the seamstress. She slipped up behind him and hugged him. "Hey, ugly," she said, "quit bothering Rose, will you?"

"Hey, uglier-than-me," he answered, returning her hug with a rib-crushing one of his own. Although he was James's older brother by five years, there was little physical similarity between them. Where James had been fair and aristocratic looking, Mike was burly and bearded. His forearms boasted tattoos of snakes and marijuana leaves, and his fingers, when laced together, spelled out a rather obscene curse. He had wild, dark blond springy hair and sharp blue eyes. Aside from his family, his passions in life were Shakespeare and his troupe of actors and actresses. On the side, he ran a motorcycle-equipment and repair shop. All in all, he was a character she found entertaining, amusing and absorbing—the older brother she'd never had. As he'd approached forty, he'd mellowed into a mainstay of the community, giving up drugs, participating in the annual Bikers' Toy Run and lending his experience to drunk-driving programs.

He looked Heather over. "You look great this morning." He raised an eyebrow with a leer. "What'd you do over the weekend?"

"None of your business, nosy. Are you ready for me, Rose?"

The seamstress, a slender, dark young woman, grinned. "I sure am. You're my favorite. Look what I have for you this time. Is it great or what?" She held up a deep blue velvet dress, cut into an Empire style with a square neckline in both front and back. Edging the bodice were gold lace and tiny pearls. The sleeves were slit down the center to display more gold lace. The pearls cascaded over the bodice and down the velvet of the sleeves.

"Oh, my!" Heather breathed, touching the dress reverently. "This is beautiful. I hope it fits." She clasped her hands. "Let me try."

It fit as if it had been made for her. She rustled the heavy fabric deliciously and regally presented herself for inspection. "What do you think?" she asked Mike and Rose.

"You look like Juliet," Mike said.

"I knew it would be great." Rose stepped forward to adjust a fold or two. "I think we'll do the same thing you've done today with your hair. I can embroider some pearls on a ribbon. What do you think?"

"I feel great in this dress," Heather enthused. "I'm going to love wearing it."

Mike crossed his arms and considered her. "I hope your Romeo finds you in it," he stated, and there was a strangely sober note in his voice.

"I'm not ready for a Romeo," she retorted, and rustled back into the dressing room.

"Yes, you are, my friend," he called after her. "You just don't know it yet."

Heather looked at him over her shoulder and stuck out her tongue before disappearing into the changing room. He'd been after her for almost two years to find a new man. He'd even gone so far as to introduce her to what he thought were suitable candidates—a single city councilman, a biker friend of his, and a teacher at the community college. None had struck even a spark in Heather's heart, but Mike kept trying. It had become a game between them.

As she dressed in her street clothes, Heather shook her head. Ben Shaw, now. He was a different story. She'd been thinking of him all morning, with a mingled sense of sadness and delicious memory spilling through her at every thought.

There was no doubt that she was at least a *little* infatuated. When she remembered his lips on hers yesterday, his mustache brushing her cheek, his warm, encompassing hug, a little ripple of something she couldn't quite identify coursed through her belly.

She returned to the other room. "Are you ready for lunch?"

"Yes. Starved," Mike said.

"Would you like to join us, Rose?" Heather asked. "We're going to Nick's."

"Sounds good, but I have too much to do. I brought a lunch with me."

"See you tonight, then."

Mike and Heather walked the several blocks to the restaurant. Mike looped his arm comfortably around her shoulder as they walked, and his down coat swished against hers. "I wish you would find somebody new," he urged seriously, as they sat down in the renovated warehouse. A waitress brought them menus.

"I will, when the time comes," Heather replied lightly.

"Spend some of that money, too. That's too much cash to be left collecting dust."

It was old ground. Heather smiled with exaggerated patience. "You could spend it, too, but you're as stubborn as your grandfather." The old man had left the money to James, the younger grandson, because Mike had been as wild as a summer storm. Heather had repeatedly tried to make Mike accept at least half the inheritance. "Your grandfather was afraid you'd spend it all on wild women and rye," she added. "You wouldn't do that now."

As if he hadn't heard, Mike continued, "You could at least travel some, get some inspiration."

"I could. But my major inspiration is that hulking monster of a forgotten mill on the horizon."

"That's another thing. When are you going to finish it?"

"I don't know," Heather replied evasively. The truth was, the piece wasn't far from completion. It lacked only a final polish—the same thing it had lacked upon James's death three years before.

"I think you're afraid of testing your true potential," Mike said, unwrapping a packet of crackers from the basket on the table. "I think you could finish it any time you liked, but then you'd have to do something with it, and somebody might notice you've got a lot more talent than anyone ever guessed."

Heather just smiled. In spite of his blustery, seemingly pushy manner, Mike had her best interests at heart. He, too, had grieved over his brother, but time had eased the pain and he wanted Heather to pick up her life—not forget James, exactly, but at least lead a normal life.

However, the problems of a wife were far different from those of a brother. How could Heather tell Mike how difficult those last few months of her marriage had been? How badly she'd failed her husband? She couldn't face another relationship until she knew she was strong enough to handle everything it might involve.

They ordered—a thick roast-beef sandwich, French fries and a cola for Mike, a spinach salad and hot tea for Heather. As the waitress departed, Heather remarked, "I met a someone on the train who was even more disgusting than you are in his addiction to sugar."

"Oh?"

Heather held up her hands and leaned over the table. "He drank cherry Kool-Aid for breakfast. Almost a quart of it. And he put three or four teaspoons of sugar in a cup of coffee."

Mike lifted his eyebrows and took a long swallow of his soda. "Who was this person?"

"Just a fellow traveler," she answered lightly. "It was nice to have someone to talk to," she went on casually, hoping to underplay her reaction to Ben. "The train was stalled for hours."

"Oh? How'd you pass all those long hours?"

"We played backgammon, as a matter of fact. He was an excellent player."

"What was this mysterious man's name, and when will you see him again?"

"Honestly, Mike. He was a stranger on a train. I'm sure I'll *never* see him again. But you might have heard of him. He writes Western novels."

"Oh yeah? What's his name?"

"Ben Shaw. I hadn't ever heard of him, but I don't read Westerns."

Mike's mouth dropped open a bit. "You met Ben Shaw on the train?"

"You know his books, then?"

"Yeah." Mike grinned and shifted in his seat. His blue eyes glinted. "I'm impressed, little sister. He's said to be quite a ladies' man."

Heather frowned. "He didn't seem like that type. He was a gentleman."

"Good. If he spent more than an hour in your company, he's done better than any other man in the last three years."

"It wasn't like that," Heather protested, but a little sting of color belied her words as she thought of the silky texture of Ben's hair and the feel of his full, sensual mouth upon hers. She swallowed to regain her composure.

Surprisingly, Mike let the subject drop with a tact that was rare for him. "Let's go over the numbers for the play. I've got the final-week jitters."

Heather appeased his doubts, as she did each season, with each play. By Friday afternoon, he would be a bear, roaring around the set, picking at costumes, scrubbing at nonexistent stains on the scenery and the floor. When the first applause sounded, he would visibly relax, and by the end of the evening his mood would be expansive and warm, and he would throw a party for the entire cast in his rambling Victorian home. It had been at just such a party that Heather had first met James. He'd been sitting in a window seat alone, as the party ebbed and flowed around him. That was a little over six years ago.

Resolutely Heather pushed the memory away and concentrated on stilling Mike's anxieties about the production.

Mike, for once, honestly felt no last-minute jitters. This whole play had a charmed air about it—the costumes and sets had fallen together perfectly. No one had canceled at the last minute, and all seven performances were selling out, three days before the first night. He voiced his usual worries and let Heather soothe him in order to give her time to let Ben Shaw recede from the conversation. As Mike thought of the name again, it took all his self-control to keep a grin the size of the Grand Canyon from spreading across his face. Ben Shaw, by damn! He nearly chortled over the delightful irony of it.

After lunch, Heather left Mike at the theater and walked downtown. She picked up some birdseed at a pet store and some tea at a specialty shop, then browsed and window-shopped down Fourth Street. On impulse, she stopped in a bookstore.

She wasn't sure what she was in the mood for, but after her rehearsal a long evening stretched ahead. Something engrossing and involving, she decided. No literature with dark themes or troubling messages or convoluted styles that would require careful unraveling, although she did read such books for the mental exercise. She paused at a collection of Longfellow's poetry and hesitated. Nope. Too thoughtful. She headed for the popular paperbacks and lingered there, picking up several and then restlessly deciding against them. She wandered down the aisle. A historical romance? She pursed her lips and skimmed the titles. Too many moments of longing, she decided. Heaven knew she had enough of her own.

When she found herself standing before the Western titles, she knew why she'd wandered into the book shop. She felt foolish standing there in front of all the melodramatic titles and briefly wondered what she would do if someone she knew saw her there. She would lie, she decided—say they were for a friend of hers.

There were more of Ben's novels in the racks than she'd expected, and their covers weren't the same as the others. Instead of featuring Indians with war-painted faces or rough-looking cowboys, the covers of Ben's books often showed a single item or a simple landscape: a carved pipe hung with feathers on an embossed cover; a hide tepee in a snowy forest grove; a horse with ribbons in its mane; a field of cultivated crops with a hoe standing alongside. As she viewed these covers, Heather felt a ripple of excitement touch her and she licked her bottom lip.

Her impulse was to buy all of them and take them home to review, one by one. That seemed somehow dangerous, though she didn't probe too closely into the reasons. She wasn't quite sure whether she was more afraid of liking or disliking the Ben that would leak through his words.

After mulling over the selection, she picked two of the novels—the one with the tepee in the snow and the one with the farm scene. They were titled respectively *A Christmas Tale* and *Finding the Circle*. Intrigued, she carried them to the counter.

"Oh, you're in for a treat," the male clerk commented as he noted her choices. "These two are a couple of his best."

"Really? Have you read many?"

"Every one, I bet. I met him, too, when he signed his books here. He's a nice man."

Heather smiled. "Really? I'll look forward to my evenings this week, then."

"We have a lot more back there when you're done with those."

"Thank you." Heather smiled and picked up her sack. On the way out, she realized she'd forgotten to say the books weren't for her.

After the rehearsal and a light dinner, she settled down with her purchases. Amadeus flew to the coffee table at her feet, whistled merrily for a moment, then quieted as she began to read.

A Christmas Tale was a fictionalized account of the massacre at Wounded Knee four days after Christmas, 1890, told from the point of view of a Dakota Indian youth on the brink of manhood. The scenes were rich with descriptive detail and with the growing romance between the young man and a girl in his tribe. Heather read eagerly, unaware of the passing hours, engrossed in the flow of Ben's writing. The tape she'd put on as background music clicked off without her noticing; her tea grew cold. Amadeus flew back to his cage, tucked his head under his wing and went to sleep next to Peter. And still Heather read, horror mounting as she began to understand what would happen.

When the violence did occur, with soldiers firing on the tribe, the brutal scene was gruesomely described. Heather felt ill with it and threw the book down in disgust—it was unnecessary, she fumed as she stomped into the kitchen, to provide every grisly detail. If all Ben's books contained that kind of violence, she wouldn't read them.

She put the kettle on for more tea and dumped her cold cup, pushing the ugly scenes to the back of her mind. And yet, even as she puttered, she felt the evocative pull of the novel like a spell over her senses, thought of the gentle Indian narrator and his passion, his love for his tribe and the land and his woman. Surely he had to survive if he was telling the story, Heather hoped. Would his woman? What would happen then? She glanced over her shoulder into the living room at the book on the couch. The war scene echoed along her nerves painfully. Since James's death, she'd refused even to read newspapers unless it was the women's section or the comics.

The water began to boil. Heather made another cup of tea and carried it into the living room. She saw her sleeping birds and ignored stereo and smiled to herself. It was a good book; she couldn't deny that. He wrote well—better than he'd led her to expect, with his casual attitude, and she liked what she could glimpse of the man through his work. She bit her lip as she paused in the middle of the room, her tea in hand. The violence might bring her nightmares back—but it might already be too late to prevent them. If the book had a redeeming end, maybe it would help allay those ugly dreams.

She was really so involved, she couldn't put the book away; that was the trouble. With a grimace of resignation, she set the tea on the coffee table, covered the birdcage, turned the tape over, and then, with a sigh, sat down to finish the novel.

The narrator *did* make it, and his woman with him, but so many of the other main characters were killed that Heather found herself weeping copiously, with an ache in her chest over the diminished lives of the people Ben had created with such grace and empathy. She was filled with unbearable sadness as she cried, burying her face in the couch.

Then, somehow, her tears were no longer being shed for the fictional creations of a stranger who had been kind to her, but for the flesh-and-blood personage of James. With an acuity she tried to avoid, she saw his face before her, with its clear blue-green eyes, the hollowness below his cheekbones, the strong nose and fine blond hair. She saw it as it had been in laughter, the night she'd first met him, flirting and playing with her. She wept in self-pity for the love she had lost; wept, too, for James himself and the sensitivity that had been his undoing.

Eventually her tears burned themselves out, and she fell asleep.

The nightmare began as always, with a cold November evening. Heather hurried home from a class she'd been teaching. All around her, brown leaves fluttered to the ground. As she drove, she took pleasure in the colors of the leaves contrasting against the gray sky, and beyond, in the steel mill rising in black and snaky splendor like a finger of the past, its stacks smokeless because of layoffs. An insight about her composition on the steel mill struck her in the sudden way of creative thoughts, and when she reached the house, she ran to the little study she kept in an alcove of her bedroom to scribble some notes.

That done, she called out to James with high pleasure, wanting to share her news.

Here the dream shifted. The hallway between her bedroom and the workroom where James made the square cedar chests that made him his living stretched into a harrowingly long tunnel, with the door to his room at the end slightly ajar. Heather walked and walked and walked, and never got any closer to the door. She called James, and the deep silence of the house echoed in her ears, becoming a roar. "James!" she cried. "James!" Her hand fell on the crystal doorknob, then Heather jerked awake, awash in sweat.

She sat up shakily and covered her face with her hands. The old, familiar guilt that she'd failed the person that she loved the most hung in her chest—a thudding ache that went too deep to be released through tears. She sighed and got up.

In the bathroom she washed her face with cool water, then looked at herself in the mirror. For a few days, she'd actually begun to think of herself as a normal person again. The freedom had been heady and delicious, but she knew now that she wasn't normal, and that if she ever tried to forget, her dreams would surely remind her. Ben, for all his kindness and his own background of pain, couldn't release her from this prison.

Even if he could, the very fact of his background would force Heather to back away. Her conscience wouldn't allow her to become involved again with a veteran who carried scars she obviously wasn't equipped to soothe or handle.

Chapter Six

Thursday, Heather found it difficult to concentrate. She had a round of private lessons to teach to grade-school children—a task she ordinarily enjoyed. This morning, her mood was infected with both the nightmare and the spell of Ben's book. She would start a lesson, begin with the child playing the piece he was to have practiced over the last week, and something about the sky would call up a scene from the book. Heather would no longer be herself, but a Dakota boy, in love and at peace with the world. Like any good book, Ben's had left behind its aura.

The other aura—one that tangled with the other—was completely different. All day, she found herself caught in the ugly cycle of *what if?* What if she hadn't put so much energy into her work and had done more for James? What if she'd left his memories and pain alone to heal by themselves rather than pushing into his life like an angry marauder? What if she'd been better prepared to deal with the horror of his wartime experience? What if she hadn't been so shocked at his confessions?

I could have adjusted, she thought. *He didn't give me a chance.*

The dress rehearsal for the play was held at five-thirty. When Heather arrived, cold and irritated by the entire day, a stage hand gave her a small package. "What's this?" Heather asked.

"A messenger delivered it. He said you should have it today."

She frowned and looked the package over. It was wrapped simply, in brown paper, with her name scrawled over the front in a slanting, spidery hand. "Did he say who sent it?"

"Sorry."

Intrigued and puzzled, Heather carried the package to her small dressing room, where the costume she was to wear for the play had been hung. At the sight of it, she felt a little of her moodiness lift. How could anyone maintain a depressed attitude wearing a dress like that? She brushed the lush velvet with her open palm and smiled.

Sitting down at the dressing table, she opened the small package carefully. When the brown paper had been removed, a white box remained, still giving no clue to its origin. She lifted the flaps to find a wad of tissue paper, and she poked around with one finger, searching for the contents. Finally she encountered something small and hard and cold, and she drew it out: a ring.

It was made of delicate cast silver. Heather held it up in wonderment. Wound around the ring was a circle of dancing elves, molded in such perfect detail that a single knee and leg of one of the elves was even extended free. She touched the tiny leg in amazement. It was the work of a skilled and playful artist. Who could have sent it?

She did occasionally receive presents from members of an audience, although they came after she'd performed. One had never come before a show.

"Hurry up, everyone!" Mike called from the hallway. "We're about ready."

Hurriedly, Heather tried to slip the ring on one of her fingers. The only place it fit was on the third finger of her left hand, so she moved her wedding ring to her right hand and put the elves on her left. Then she quickly undressed and donned her costume.

Halfway through, she had to call for the seamstress to help her lace up the dress. "Good thing these women all had ladies' maids," she joked when Rose joined her.

Rose agreed. "But they'd never heard of zippers in those days, so count your blessings."

The dress rehearsal went well, and afterward Heather headed home. It hadn't been intentional, but when she'd played that evening, her fingers on the guitar had found the most melancholy chords. She had no appetite and no desire to sleep. Around her, the house echoed hollowly. For one brief moment, she thought of selling it and reinvesting, of living somewhere else. This house had too many memories—both good and bad. Sometimes the very air seemed to be infected with the past.

This thought made her feel even guiltier. At the very least, she could hang on to the house that had meant so much to James. It was a small thing and the only thing she had left to give.

The first showing of *Twelfth Night* was to be performed on Halloween—a fact that had worried a number of people involved in the production. There had been no way to exchange the times with those of other events scheduled at the arts center, so reluctantly Mike had agreed to keep the date. He peeked out at the gathering crowd Friday night with renewed hope. As he scanned the faces of the well-dressed audience, he was gratified to see a wide range of people—not only the usual core of wealthy, white supporters in their forties and fifties, but a generous sprinkling of youthful and brown-to-black faces, as well. The audience was animated, calling and chatting in the aisles, admiring one another's finery and catching up on gossip. Mike nodded to himself. Perhaps, after seven years, he was beginning to build a name for himself and his troupe. The lights dimmed slightly and he hurried into the hallways of dressing rooms below the ascending seats.

"Is everybody ready?" he called, clapping his hands. A flurry of yeses reached him. He checked to confirm the reality of their claims, then, with clammy hands, brushed the costume he wore for effect. He ran onstage and called to one of the flower girls selling long-stemmed roses to the audience. "Lady, be so kind as to carry a rose to my wife." The audience loved it. A good sign.

Now his only worry was Heather. He ran to her dressing room to find her fully costumed, looking spectacularly right for the period in her breathtaking velvet gown. Her long golden braid was wrapped with pearls and more velvet. "You look fabulous," he cried, kissing her cheek. "I wish you would think of taking a small part in one of these plays. No one looks more Shakespearean than you do."

She smiled dutifully, but under the makeup she was pale, and her movements were mechanical. Nightmares again, he thought. He would bet on it. For the thousandth time, he cursed his brother. Mike had hoped that the meeting with Ben Shaw would chase away some of Heather's self-doubt, cancel her long punishment. He'd glimpsed a new light in her eyes over lunch the other day—a light that was now gone.

Heather leaned into the mirror, mentally rehearsing the first chords of the opening piece. She adjusted the heavy cast-silver tree that hung from a strong silver chain around her neck. It had come that afternoon by messenger to the arts center. Again, there had been no note—just the gnarled tree, magnificently designed. In spite of the mystery of its origin, she couldn't resist wearing it. "Are you sure you didn't send this, Michael?"

"It wasn't me, I swear." He grinned through his beard. "You must have a secret admirer."

She nodded thoughtfully. The three-inch tree had the same kind of artistic detail and spirit as the ring she'd received the day before. She bit her lip as a fragment of conversation came back to her. Ben had called her Titania. Could he have sent the spectacular jewelry?

But how would he know where to find her? And why would he go through the trouble of sending a messenger instead of delivering it himself? No. It had to be someone else—perhaps one of her students.

"Are we about ready?" she asked Mike.

"You can go out any time."

"I'm on my way." She picked up her guitar and patted her clothing down one more time. "Break a leg," she said as she exited her room.

She waited in the wings for Mike's signal to the light man, and as the house dimmed, she straightened her spine and took her place on the stage, on a chair to one side of the set where she would remain throughout the performance. It was good exposure for her work and a chance to perform as a musician to a larger audience. Of all her jobs, this one gave her the most pleasure. She also knew that her guitar playing had become a trademark of Mike's theatrical productions.

She strummed the first chords, an introduction to attune the audience, and heard the people settle in their seats around her, sighs of anticipation whispering from them, the sound like hundreds of birds landing softly on a tree. Heather, too, felt her dark mood melt away as the music sang over her frayed nerves. The actors and actresses for the first scene assembled themselves onstage, and soon Heather was completely lost in the artistic expression of the play.

It went well. The timing was beyond anyone's expectations and some of the actors who had begun with the company as amateurs were coming into their own, showing fuller powers of interpretation. The audience laughed and quieted. Out of the corner of her eye, Heather saw some of them sitting forward in absorption, and she smiled to herself. The party at Mike's house tonight would be a rollicking one.

At the happy end of the play, Heather stood with the others to take a bow before the wildly applauding and cheering audience. She curtsied with the other women, her guitar in hand, and flowers pelted them, falling on the stage in a boisterous, spontaneous display of approval. She grinned at the actress next to her and they ran offstage.

Mike was in the wings, meeting each player with a monstrous hug. When Heather's turn came, he swept her completely off her feet and swung her around with a great laugh. "You outdid yourself tonight, my girl!" he exclaimed. "You were fantastic!"

"Thank you."

She made her way through the cluster of people and escaped to the small room she had to herself. In the mirror of the big dressing table, her face was flushed and her eyes sparkled. The gown, she thought, was magnificent. Too bad people didn't wear things like this anymore. She twirled to feel the weighty pull of the velvet against her legs.

The heady rush of anticipation for the future that she'd felt on the train touched her again, chasing away the residue of her nightmare. Tonight, she was free. She would wear her glorious dress this evening to the party and then at the performances tomorrow and all next week.

In the mirror a pair of booted feet appeared at her door, and Heather turned with a smile, expecting Mike. Instead, to her consternation, she saw Ben Shaw standing in the doorway, a half grin tilting his mustache to one side. "Hi," he said simply.

For a moment, Heather couldn't speak. He was even more handsome than she'd remembered. The dark waves of his hair gleamed in the low light of the hallway behind him, and his fathomless eyes shone with humor. Tonight he was dressed in black corduroy with a white shirt and patterned tie in red and black. The slacks fit his long legs snugly, and the tailored jacket attractively emphasized his wide shoulders. Unconsciously, she took in a sudden breath at the impact of his appearance. "Hello, Ben."

Without taking his gaze from her, he stepped into the room, closing the distance between them. "I haven't thought about anything but you since Tuesday." He touched the tree at her neck. "Do you like it?"

"It was you? How did you know where to find me?"

He grinned at her question, dropping his hand. "There can't be too many places a classical guitarist could perform for a play in Pueblo. I called around until I found out where *Twelfth Night* was going to be." He quickly lifted an eyebrow.

"It's beautiful, Ben," she said sincerely. "So is the ring." She lifted her hand to show it to him. Embarrassed to reveal that it was on her wedding-ring finger, she added, "That was the only finger it fit."

"Pretty," he remarked. "I saw them at a crafts fair in the mountains the day after we got back. I couldn't resist them." He took her hand and kissed the knuckles. His fingers were strong and lean, like the rest of him; his sensual lips firm on her flesh. Again, her breath fled and she drank deeply of his face with her eyes.

He straightened and took another step toward her. "You look beautiful tonight," he said with a smile and touched her cheek.

Heather's gaze was frozen on the wonderful planes of his face. Until he'd appeared, she hadn't known how badly she wanted to see him again, and now that he was here, it was difficult not to throw herself into his arms at the reprieve. "Thank you." She realized she was staring like a love-struck fourteen-year-old, and found her voice. "It's good to see you."

His deep brown eyes shone. "You, too." He smiled. "Are you free tonight?"

"There's a party at the director's house, to celebrate the play. I'm really required to be there for a while. We might go get something to eat later, though."

His dark eyes shone. "That sounds nice."

"Heather, you ready?" Mike called from the hallway, stopping in his tracks when he entered the room. "Oh, sorry. I didn't know you had a visitor."

Ben turned. "Hello, Mike. Long time no see."

"Ben!" Mike slapped Ben's shoulder. "Damn, man, why don't I ever see you anymore?"

"I gave up that life-style."

Mike laughed. "Me, too. Amazing how your perspective changes as you get older."

Throughout this exchange, Heather had been staring at the two of them in disbelief. "You two know one another?"

"You better believe it." Mike threw an arm around the other man's shoulders. "This was the best bareback rider in all of high-school rodeo in 1970. He won the national prize."

Ben winced. "Take it easy braggin' up the year, man."

"Are you coming to the house?"

"Yes," Heather answered. "I invited him to come with me."

Mike gave her a long look and she lifted her chin under his scrutiny. He was the one who'd been urging her to date again. Now he would have his wish.

"I'll see you there, then."

As he left, Ben turned to Heather with a serious expression in his eyes. "Is that going to make a difference, my knowing Mike?"

Heather smiled. "No. I'm glad you know him." Surprisingly, as she uttered the words, she found them to be true.

"How did you two hook up?" Ben asked.

"He's—he was . . ." Heather frowned. How did the tense work when the brother that made someone a sister-in-law was no longer living? "His brother was my husband. Did you know James, as well?"

"Not really. He was younger than we were." Ben took her hand and laced his fingers through hers. "Your name sounded familiar, but I couldn't place just why. I always forget Mike and James had different last names." He turned twinkling eyes on her. "Now if you'd said your name was Heather Milisavljevich, I would have known who you were."

"I've been with Mike often enough when he had to spell that three times," Heather said. "At least people usually get Scarborough in one spelling." His fingers felt hard and strong against hers. "Are you ready to go? I'll drive."

In the car, neither of them spoke much. Ben seemed huge in the little vehicle, and she was acutely conscious of his leathery scent. "You can smoke if you like," she said. "I don't mind."

"Thanks, but I can't smoke in a nonsmoker's car. It takes forever for the smell to go away."

Heather added another virtue to her list of his qualities—consideration. So far, there was only one negative, but it was a big one. Wait and see, she reprimanded herself. At least give the guy a chance. But was it to Ben or herself she was giving a chance? That was a question she wasn't ready to answer.

Mike's house, not far from the theater and just north of downtown, was set amid huge elms and cottonwoods. It had been in desperate need of repair when Mike, his wife Ellen and their three children had moved in two years ago. Now, thanks to Ellen's carpentry skills, the porch was sturdy and gleaming, the staircase had been stripped of its paint and varnished, and the crumbling plaster over the brick fireplace in the living room had been removed. Mike had traded electrical wiring for rebuilding a rare old motorcycle and although the plumbing was still reliable, it was slowly being replaced, one bit at a time.

Tonight, huge jack-o'-lanterns glowed at each corner of the porch. From within, a lilting medieval song spilled out into the night, and laughter reached Ben and Heather on the sidewalk. "Sounds like someone is having fun in there," Ben commented, taking her arm.

"You sound like you aren't sure *you* will."

He shrugged. "I'll be glad to be with you, but parties never have been something I liked a lot."

Heather felt the same way, but she was surprised that Ben did. He seemed sociable and outgoing. "Why?"

"I don't dance. I don't drink. And I have trouble with small talk." He glanced at her, a whisper of a smile on his lips. "That about covers party action."

"To tell you the truth, I feel exactly the same way. But Mike would be crushed if we didn't go for a little while. We'll leave early and go have something to eat. Okay?"

In answer, he squeezed her arm and they entered the house, strangely united.

Ellen greeted them dressed in her costume, a rich topaz velvet with a brocaded bodice. She held a major part in every one of Mike's plays—a fact that caused some dissent among the other members of the troupe. Tonight she'd played Olivia, and had done it magnificently. Her eyes widened at the sight of Heather and Ben—more at Ben, Heather noted. "Come in, you two. Can I get you a drink?"

"Coffee, Ellen." Heather glanced at Ben with a smile. "And plenty of sugar."

"Sure. You know Mike." She shrugged expressively. "I'll get you some."

"That's all right," Heather said. "You go enjoy your party. I know the way to the kitchen."

"Oh, I don't mind." Ellen ushered them through the wide arches of living and dining rooms, through knots of people chatting about the play and dancing a ritualized step from the Middle Ages.

"Now, that's a dance step I might be able to handle," Ben murmured to Heather.

"It's kind of fun. I learned it for another play."

His voice dropped even lower, taking on an intimate note. "Maybe you could teach me sometime."

She half smiled and dipped her head.

The kitchen was crowded, but Ellen good-naturedly elbowed a path through the people to the coffee maker. Mike stood there, a mug in his hand, chatting with a younger man whose haircut looked familiar to Heather. Mike caught sight of the trio heading his way and threw a friendly arm around the other man. "Tom. I'd like you to meet Heather Scarborough, Ben Shaw and my wife, Ellen."

Heather smiled at the young man. "We've met. What a nice surprise, Tom." He was the student who'd shown both talent and perseverance in learning the difficult guitar piece for class earlier in the week.

He colored, so that his fair skin showed a mottling of red from his jaw to his eyes. He nodded shyly at each of them.

Heather noted his shyness with interest. While he played the guitar, he was relaxed, at home, unselfconscious—even more of an indication that he was a natural talent. What held him back? She made a mental note to ask Mike about Tom's background. Perhaps it would contain some clue that would help her to convince the guitarist to pursue his gift.

Now she poured a cup of coffee for herself and Ben. "Sugar, Mike?"

He grabbed a squat bowl. Heather passed it to Ben with a smile. The brown eyes glittered in amusement. "I'm touched you remember."

"It's difficult to forget that much sugar in one cup of coffee."

Mike looked at Ben. "So, you went out and got yourself famous? I've read all your books, man. You're good."

"Thanks. That means a lot, coming from you. You must've read every book in the school library."

Heather's eyebrows flew as she glanced at her brother-in-law. "You were a bookworm?"

Ben laughed, and his hand touched the small of her back, comforting and warm. "More like a rebel worm. He'd come to school all dressed in black leather, with his hair grown way past decency, then sit on his motorcycle in the parking lot, reading."

"I was so self-consciously rebellious," Mike admitted ruefully. "It embarrasses me now."

Heather had laughed with the others at the strangely acute picture of Mike as a teenager. "What was Ben like?"

Mike shook his head. "I wish I could say he was weird in some way, but he wasn't. He rode rodeos, but he wasn't a redneck. He played basketball, but he wasn't a stuck-up jock. He made the honor role every semester, but he never said a word about it, and he didn't spend all his time in the library, either.'' Mike looked at Ben with admiration. ''He was always cool in high school. Later... Now that was a different story.''

''And one we won't go into just now, if you don't mind. I'm on my best behavior.'' Ben slipped his hand into Heather's. ''She promised to teach me a dance.''

Just before he pulled her away, Heather looked at Tom. ''I want you to find a new piece to play for me next week, okay?''

''I'd like to learn one of yours, if you'd let me.''

''I'd be honored. I'll bring some with me to class.''

He nodded solemnly. Heather followed Ben into the other room.

The dancers had paused, so Heather and Ben took seats near the bay window in the candlelit room to watch the other festivities. Ellen led a bobbing contest, and came up with an apple caught between her small white teeth. For a moment she paused, dancing to the flutes and drums in the background as the gathered merrymakers cheered.

''What was it you didn't want Mike to tell me in there?'' Heather asked.

He wiggled his nose and smiled. ''Nothing much. Just that I was a real hell-raiser for a while when I got back home from Vietnam.''

"I'm disappointed," she teased, amazed even as she said it that she could be so natural with him. "I was hoping for something dramatic and exciting."

He grinned at her. "Nope."

For a long stretch of seconds, Heather fell adrift in his eyes, seeing suddenly very deeply into his soul, perceiving a complex man with pains and joys and sorrows and hopes that she wanted very much to learn about. She dropped her eyes, confused by that wish. Until a week ago, she hadn't known he existed.

"What were *you* like in high school, Heather?"

"Oh, very studious and quiet. One of those wall-flower girls no one ever notices."

"I can't believe that. I would have noticed you, I bet."

"No," she said regretfully. "You would have noticed Ellen."

"Wrong. I didn't develop a taste for women like that until a whole lot later." His fingers, soft and whispery and sensual, moved slowly over Heather's forearm. "In high school, I had more sense. I liked smart girls with something they cared about outside of me."

Heather smiled faintly, but didn't believe him. Suddenly a question occurred to her. "Where do you live, anyway, Mr. Shaw?"

He grinned, showing his white teeth below the mustache. "In Beulah."

Beulah was a small town at the foot of the Rockies, thirty miles outside Pueblo. She nodded. "I, um, did buy one of your books. Well, actually two, but I haven't read the second one yet."

Ben became abruptly still, poised for her response. Observing the action, Heather realized that Ben cared a great deal about his work, despite what he said.

But when he spoke, his voice was even, casually interested. "Which ones?"

"*A Christmas Tale.* The second one was *Finding the Circle.*"

He nodded but didn't meet her eyes. Somehow his reaction touched Heather deeply. "You didn't tell me you were such a fine writer."

His sable gaze met hers slowly. "Don't say anything you don't mean, Heather."

"I'm not." She sighed. "I didn't like the violence. In fact, I nearly quit reading it when I got to the massacre. And it gave me nightmares." She let go a short, humorless laugh. "Or rather, it brought back my old friends."

"I know a little about nightmares," he said. "I get rid of mine on the pages of those books. It's good therapy. Maybe the same thing would work with your music."

Heather doubted it. Composing had been difficult since James's death. "Maybe," she replied without much hope. Her attention shifted to the dancers, who were assembled for the dance Ben had liked. "Would you still like to try that one? We have room in our corner here. We don't have to join them.''

"Sure.'' He set his coffee cup on a nearby table and stood, offering his hand to help her up.

She paused for a moment to listen to the music, and looked at Ben. "We face one another like this.'' Her hands were buried in the soft velvet of her skirt, and she curtsied deeply. "Now, two steps backward, two steps to the side. All very slowly.''

Ben mimicked her with surprising grace, his face showing a faint smile.

"Now, two steps forward and we circle, palm to palm.'' She pressed her palm to his and her gaze caught his lips. "Now the other palm the other way.'' Her voice dropped to a murmur as he complied. The room dropped away. She imagined they stood in a castle great-room, dancing within the stone walls as torchlight flickered over his hair. "Now, two steps back, turn, turn back, and we meet with both palms.'' As their hands met, Heather felt a jolt of electricity travel through her arms, landing in a pool in her stomach. Her heart thumped in her throat as she looked up into his face. "Now we repeat the whole thing,'' she said softly.

He had a facile memory, for he followed her directions without missing a step. When they came together for the first circle, his gaze held hers. "You are so beautiful, Heather,'' he murmured.

The gentle smile was gone from his eyes, and in its place was a sultry glimmer that made her breath catch. Her pulse surged erratically through her body as she turned to offer her other hand. The music and the ritual of the ancient dance made the touch of their palms an intensely intimate gesture, and each time she reached up to press his hand, Heather felt her skin leaping with greater and greater sensitivity until her palms nearly burned when they met both of his. Her breathing felt as if it were a thing apart from her and this moment wrapped in the music with Ben.

When they'd completed a full round of steps, Ben paused, pinning her with his look. He slid his hands over hers, creating a subtle, delicious friction. His gaze steadily probed Heather's. His palms were firm and supple and strong, and the sensation he created with his simple movement was one of the most erotic Heather had ever experienced. When the music ended with a shout from the other dancers, she was shattered out of her reverie and snatched her hands away, but her gaze was still fastened upon his. He reached up to touch her face, cupping her chin, and his lips edged toward hers. When at last they closed on her mouth, Heather felt a flush of something new within her— something she didn't want to examine. She sighed against his lips, warm and strong, with the feel of his mustache a delightful accent to the sensations flooding her senses.

Except for his hand on her chin and his lips on hers, no part of their bodies touched at all. Heather almost stepped forward to him when she remembered where they were—in the very room where she'd met James. Flustered, she pulled away. "I'm not ready for this," she whispered in consternation.

Ben took her hand. "Maybe not," he said, his voice husky. He smoothed a wisp of hair away from her face. "I have lots of time." Glancing over his shoulder at the people beginning to show the high spirits of good beer and a good time, he added, "I think I'm ready to go get something to eat. Do you think you've been here long enough?"

"Oh, yes. I just needed to make an appearance. We can go now."

"How do you feel about pizza?"

Heather smiled, feeling herself return to normal. "Now, that's one junk food I love." She looked at her dress. "I want to change my clothes before we go anywhere else, though."

"Okay. It's early, yet. We can run by your house first."

She said her goodbyes and they departed. As they drove, it started to snow very lightly. "I hope this doesn't get any worse," Heather noted grimly.

"You don't like the snow?"

"I just hate to drive in it. It scares me half to death. Basically, I just don't, period."

Ben smiled. "We'll be all right." He wanted to reach out and pat her hand, but both of them were firmly placed at ten and two o'clock on the steering wheel. She leaned slightly forward to see out the windshield. At the mere sight of snow, her shoulder muscles had tensed. "Why are you so afraid of bad weather?"

"When I was seventeen I slid my car right into the side of a bridge. It turned out all right because I wasn't going very fast, but it could have been terrible. All I did was break my arm."

"Nobody likes slippery roads."

"I'm not nobody or most people," she countered stiffly. "When it gets icy, I just don't drive." A little flicker of wry humor twisted her lips into the semblance of a smile. "I don't know why they invented cars at all. I hate driving."

Ben laughed. "You just get somebody to drive you around. That's what I do."

"Is that how you got to Pueblo tonight?"

"Sure is."

"Maybe I'll see if I can find someone willing to trade time at the wheel for guitar lessons," Heather suggested, smiling.

"I have to pay John, but you're prettier than I am." Her perfume wafted over him—a scent reminiscent of cloves and cinnamon. His gaze traveled over the oval of her face to the pale flesh just below her ear. The dress left a good portion of her shoulder bare, and without conscious thought he reached out to touch the vulnerable spot. Beneath the satiny texture of her skin, a muscle hard with tension resisted his fingers. "God, woman, you're as wound up as a cat."

"I never sleep well when I'm having my nightmares."

"What kind of nightmares do you have?" He rubbed the muscle absently, taking pleasure in simply touching her, in watching the snow-muted light play over her medieval-looking face.

"Just one." She swallowed. "But I don't like to talk about it. No offense."

"None taken." He slid his fingers up her neck to the curve of her jaw. He knew from the papers that James had committed suicide, and he had a hunch her nightmares had something to do with that. But three years was a long time for a widow to grieve.

She pulled into the driveway of a sturdy brick home. Along the side lining the asphalt, three panels of wide glass brick broke the solid facade. "You have a fortress, here."

"They definitely built these houses to last."

"I would have pictured you in something different," Ben commented as they climbed out of the car.

"Really?" She smiled faintly, cloaked in the odd distance she sometimes adopted. "Like what?"

"Like a house of trees." He grinned and was rewarded with a genuine smile.

He followed her into the darkened living room and stayed close to the door until she flicked on the lights.

With his luck, he would stumble into some priceless heirloom.

"It'll only take a moment for me to change," she said. "Make yourself at home."

"All right."

In her bedroom, Heather paused a moment to catch her breath. Her cheeks were hot and her stomach seemed alive with electricity. She turned on a small crystal lamp on her dresser. In the full-length mirror, her cheeks were flushed and her eyes glowed with blue excitement. Beauty, she thought with a smile. Ben Shaw had given her some beauty.

Behind her in the living room, she heard him talking softly to the birds. Amadeus answered cheerfully and even Peter, bad-tempered as he was, chirped in reply. She moved toward the door, beginning to unfasten the button at the top of her gown, then remembered with dismay the complicated ties at the back. Her words to the seamstress about ladies' maids came back to her mockingly.

Briefly she considered not changing her clothes, after all, rather than ask Ben for assistance; but the thought of struggling with the same problem later, decided her. "Ben?"

"Yes?"

"I need a little help, if you wouldn't mind."

He appeared from around the corner, a rakish expression tilting his mustache. "Sure thing, little lady." An unruly dark wave of hair fell over his forehead and he brushed it away. Heather felt the wattage in her belly leap.

"It's, um, these ties in the back." She turned to show him. She felt his approach in the change that suddenly rippled over her body, as if he carried a chemical aura of tinder that kindled her inner cells. She licked her lips. "If you'll just untie those, I can probably manage the rest." She lifted her braid and pulled it over one shoulder.

He lifted his hands to the ties and did as he'd been asked. "Is that all you wanted?"

Heather nodded, unable to speak.

Ben stepped closer and placed his hands on her shoulders. The smooth pads of his fingers on her bare flesh jolted her and she started. He tightened his fingers slightly. "Relax," he murmured into her ear. The moist and heated air of his breath drifted over the delicate skin below her ear. When he flickered his tongue over the lobe of her ear, Heather gasped. For one fleeting second, a warning signal flashed in her mind, a sound like a smoke alarm, but his breath flowed over her skin and she couldn't move—not yet. In a minute, she promised herself. In a minute or two she would bring them both back to reality.

As if weighted, her eyelids slipped shut and she swayed back, leaning into his chest. A languorous thudding pulsed heavily in her lips and belly and breasts. Ben's mouth moved over her neck and whispered over the corner of her jaw, and his hair brushed her shoulder as he circled her waist with his hands. His voice, as dark and sweet as molasses, dripped in her ear, speaking her name. He pulled her tightly against him.

She knew she should stop him now, as she felt the slow heat migrating through her limbs. Instead she found herself lifting her arms to touch the deep-gloss waves of his hair, delighting in the springy texture that leaped to embrace her knuckles. Ben pressed kisses along her cheek, his tongue, bold and searing, flickering out at intervals to tease the corner of her eye or the sweep of her cheekbone. She dropped her head backward to his shoulder. He moaned softly, a lazy sound that vibrated through her bones like currents of electricity that consumed her to the core.

He moved his hands with agonizing slowness, embracing her quivering belly and rib cage, where he stopped to caress the length of each bone as he passed it. At last his palms gained the lower swell of her breasts beneath the pearls and heavy velvet. He paused and shifted Heather in his arms so that she was half turned toward him, braced in one powerful arm while he left his other hand where it lay, gently resting below her breast.

"Look at me, Heather," he demanded in a gravelly voice.

Her eyelids fluttered open. His sultry mouth took hers, his gaze trapping Heather's in a mesmeric spell. As if drawn by a magnetic field, his hand gravitated to cover her breast, finding and stroking the taut peak that seemed to strain toward the heat of his palm.

It was the most erotic, consuming moment of her life. His half-opened eyes probed hers, his tongue plundered her mouth and his hand performed an exquisite dance of expert sensuality over her breast. She imagined she could hear the sizzle of unleashed voltage and gave herself up to him, all reason overcome. No moment, past, present or future, mattered save this one.

"You smell so good," he said softly bringing his mouth to her neck. He left a trail of kisses over her collarbone, up her throat, and back down to the square of her chest revealed by the bodice of her gown.

All at once, she felt her gown give way, and she nearly bolted. Ben's mouth suddenly upon her own, teasing with tongue and lips, halted her. As his kiss invited her to sink back into the hazy sensuality of the moment, she found herself giving freely to him, her tongue conducting an exploration of its own, her heart pounding to the rhythm of his blood rushing through the vein beneath her fingers.

Ben left her mouth to feather kisses over her temple and ear and jaw, then falling to burn the upper swell of her bosom. He slid his hands steadily to their goal, expertly circling her small breasts with nimble fingertips.

Enflamed now, Heather took one step away from him. The crackling of electricity through her veins

NO COST! NO OBLIGATION TO BUY!
NO PURCHASE NECESSARY!

PLAY "LUCKY 7"
AND GET AS MANY AS SIX FREE GIFTS . .

HOW TO PLAY:

1. With a coin, carefully scratch off the silver box at the right. This makes you eligible to receive one or more free books, and possibly other gifts, depending on what is revealed beneath the scratch-off area.

2. You'll receive brand-new Silhouette Special Edition® novels. When you return this card, we'll send you the books and gifts you qualify for *absolutely free*!

3. Unless you tell us otherwise, every month we'll send you 6 additional novels to read and enjoy. If you decide to keep them, you'll pay only $2.74* per book—that's 21¢ less per book than the cover price! And $2.74 per book is all you pay! There is *no* charge for shipping and handling. There are no hidden extras.

4. When you subscribe to Silhouette Reader Service™, we'll also send you additional free gifts from time to time, as well as our newsletter.

5. You must be completely satisfied. You may cancel at any time simply by writing "cancel" on your statement or returning a shipment of books to us at our cost.

*Terms and prices subject to change without notice. Sales tax applicable in N.Y. and Iowa.
© 1989 HARLEQUIN ENTERPRISES LIMITED

You'll love your elegant bracelet watch—this classic LCD Quartz Watch is a perfect expression of your style and good taste—and it is yours FREE as an added thanks for giving our Reader Service a try.

PLAY "LUCKY 7"

Just scratch off the silver box with a coin.
Then check below to see which gifts you get.

YES! I have scratched off the silver box. Please send me all the gifts for which I qualify. I understand I am under no obligation to purchase any books, as explained on the opposite page.

235 CIS R1YE
(U-S-SE-10/89)

NAME

ADDRESS   APT

CITY   STATE   ZIP

7	7	7	WORTH FOUR FREE BOOKS, FREE BRACELET WATCH AND MYSTERY BONUS
🍒	🍒	🍒	WORTH FOUR FREE BOOKS AND MYSTERY BONUS
●	●	●	WORTH FOUR FREE BOOKS
🔔	🔔	🍒	WORTH TWO FREE BOOKS

DETACH AND MAIL CARD TODAY

BUSINESS REPLY CARD

FIRST CLASS MAIL   PERMIT NO. 717   BUFFALO, NY

Postage will be paid by addressee

SILHOUETTE BOOKS
901 FUHRMANN BLVD
PO BOX 1867
BUFFALO NY 14240-9952

NO POSTAGE
NECESSARY
IF MAILED
IN THE
UNITED STATES

filled her body with a roaring noise that canceled everything except his dangerously sensual eyes—eyes that watched as she reached up with her hands to the shoulders of her dress, slipping first one, then the other from her body. She let the heavy fabric slide away, leaving only her thin lacy slip as a shield between his eyes and her breasts.

Languorously, helplessly, Ben reached toward the aroused points, his fingers caressing them simultaneously with a touch as light as a summer breeze. While she watched, her chest rising and falling with her quick breathing, he dipped his dark head to taste her rigid nubs through the silk, using his tongue to scald them with loving spirals. She gasped.

An answering groan escaped his lips and he pulled Heather roughly into the crook of his arm, pushing away the slippery material to devour the bared white flesh of her breasts with undisciplined hunger. She ran her fingers through the silky hair at his crown and arched to meet his mouth as he traced the sensitive skin of her breasts and the valley between. A wave of dizziness engulfed her, and Ben, sensing it, moved her to the bed a few feet away, pausing only a second in his ministrations to make her comfortable.

Heather slid her fingers from the hair at his neck to the lean plane of his cheek. It was exhilarating to feel the sturdy warmth of a man against her, to feel his arms securely fastened around her, to smell his heady and alien scent. She slipped her hands down to rest upon his shoulders, strong and broad beneath the fine corduroy of his jacket. She could sense the restraint he exercised, the care he used to handle her; and a little part of her sang with it. Here, she thought breathlessly, was a man of men—gentle and strong all at once.

He brought his mouth to hers and she thrilled at the unaccustomed roughness of corduroy and cotton against her chest. The kiss deepened and Heather heard a small sound escape her as he used his tongue to urge hers into the most ancient of dances, a dance he led with consummate grace. Heather pressed into him and a jolt of excitement coursed through her as she felt his arousal and realized she was the source of it.

He kissed her urgently, his mustache bristling into the tender skin of her upper lip. Heather felt the dryness of her soul fill to overflowing as she ran her hands over his back and sides, finding at last the buttons on his shirt. She freed enough of them to let her explore the heated skin below, his chest with its covering of crisp hair, and the supple flesh of his belly. A long low sound of satisfaction emanated from deep in his throat.

He paused above her for a moment, and he laid an open palm alongside her cheek. Heather flickered her eyes open at his slowed pace to find his gaze upon her. The long-lashed eyes held an earthiness she hadn't glimpsed there before, and he kissed her, still holding her gaze, taking a sweet sip of her lips. He sighed a little raggedly and slipped his hand from her face to encircle one breast gently. He looked at the swell of flesh in his hand, then back to her face and moved his hand back to her waist. "I'm not going to make love with you yet, Heather." He glanced around the room. "And I'm not ever going to do it here."

Heather blinked. Beneath her fingers, she could feel the hard pounding of his heart, and even through the layers of velvet over her thighs there was no mistaking his desire for her. She looked at his lean face, at the planes of his high cheekbones and the exotic shape of his eyes. Even as her pulse and breathing slowed and the taut sensation in her abdomen relaxed, she knew she wanted Ben to make love with her. She wanted to join with him, learn every nuance of his movements and voice and mouth. She swallowed. "I understand."

He dipped for one last kiss, pulling the pearl-studded bodice over her breasts, then rose to straighten his clothes. "I'll wait out here."

Ben exited as gracefully as he could and closed the door behind him. In the dim hallway, he took a deep breath, cursing himself under his breath. All that resolve, all that caution, thrown to the wind the moment he could lay his hands on her. What was wrong with him? She wasn't one of the all-too-friendly women he met around town or on tours—a long way from it. He knew she needed caution and slow movement.

But she'd flared like a match at his touch, and the transformation of the shy, introverted woman into one of such genuine passion had inflamed him, as well. She was ready for a lover, but he didn't want her simply responding to him out of a need for sexual fulfillment. Ben wanted her to see *him*—not the ghost of her husband, or a fantasy man. She couldn't know or trust him well enough yet. When the moment came, he wanted the two of them to join with their eyes wide open. Because he was a man of instinct, he didn't stop to reason out his feelings. All he knew was that it was essential that they didn't rush or pretend with one another.

Rather than be caught outside her door when she finished changing, he moved down the hallway. A closed door was at the end of the passage and Ben wondered curiously what was behind it. A workroom, perhaps? He stepped toward it, moving his shoulders restlessly, an odd tightness in his neck. The pet birds, who'd been chattering at one another for the past minute, set up a racket of whistles and chirps and high protestations. A fight, Ben thought, and he grinned.

The grin faded as a puff of air whooshed in his ears, and he belatedly realized the warning of his stiff neck. He had time enough to take hold of the door handle before the edges of his vision lit with the hated halo of light.

In the dark hallway, he had little to focus upon, nothing to fasten his eyes and mind upon to ease the onslaught of the seizure, so he prepared himself for the worst. The unwelcome tingling spread through his body, blocking all outward perceptions. Just before his mind turned in upon itself, he heard Heather call his name. A moment earlier, and he might have been able to will his attention toward her. But it was too late.

His last seizure had been on the train, the day he'd first seen Heather. It had been mild, gently focused upon her medieval beauty.

This time he simply knew nothing until the halo of light blinding him grew into a sun with speckled black at the edges and Ben felt the tingling slip away from his body. Only a minute more . . . a minute.

When he returned to himself, he was sitting on the floor. Heather crouched near him, her huge eyes showing terror. "Are you all right?"

He couldn't speak, but bile rose in his belly and he struggled to his feet, shaking off Heather's attempt to help him. His entire body trembled in the aftermath and he lurched into the bathroom, slamming the door behind him. He rid himself of the bitterness and rinsed his mouth, moving carefully on rubbery legs. Every muscle in his body quivered. The look he gave his pale face in the mirror reflected the self-loathing he felt. Hell! he thought. Hellfire and damnation— Heather's thin voice came through the door. "Ben? Are you all right?"

He had no right to leave her out there, no right to hide his shame and embarrassment behind the door while she wondered over his sanity and his health. He had to face her, once again, and apologize for his cursed weakness. A voice deep in his mind cackled at his feeble attempts at creating a normal relationship.

He faced his reflection, straightening his shoulders. No. He wouldn't cringe, not even for Heather. She could take him or leave him, as he was. He opened the door.

Heather stood in the hallway, dressed in a soft green sweater with long sleeves and a pair of jeans. The pale gold braid, still laced with velvet and pearls, hung over one shoulder. She remained silent as he emerged, limping rather obviously, and she'd arranged her features into a carefully neutral mask. "Are you all right?"

Her distant concern somehow rekindled his earlier embarrassment and thus his defensiveness. "Fine," he bit out, and brushed past her into the living room. He stood there, feeling smothered by the heavy sturdiness of the rooms around him. A part of him recognized the wash of irritability as an expected portion of his seizures, but the irritation itself swept away any sense of reason he might have summoned. "I have to get out of here," he muttered. "Can I use your phone?"

"Sure." Her voice showed her perplexity. Ben didn't look at her. When she spoke again, her tone was cool and polite. "It's right over here."

A shred of sanity settled on him just as he picked up the phone. "I'm in no shape to go anywhere now." Although he'd tried to gentle his voice, it sounded harsh. "I'm going to call for a ride home."

Something wounded showed in her eyes an instant before an opaque shutter slammed down. "No explanation is necessary. I understand."

Ben reached John and gave him a message that would let him know why Ben needed him, then gave him Heather's address. After he'd hung up, he turned to look at Heather. She'd busied herself with sprinkling food over the fish tank, and didn't look up. Ben limped to the couch and sat down with a sigh.

"Can I get you something?" she asked.

Ben shook his head and Heather went to the kitchen. He heard her fill a kettle with water. He knew he was behaving badly, but his legs felt frozen and heavy, and any words of apology he might have found were buried beneath his shame. He sensed Heather's confusion, and yet the silence continued to stretch between them, thick and cloudy. It began to annoy him. "Don't you have any music in this place?"

Without speaking, Heather moved to the stereo and flipped it on. Then she went back to the kitchen to pour a cup of tea.

Under the long-cultivated barrier of polite acquiescence to a guest's wishes, Heather was seething with rage and hurt. He was being just like James. She re-membered well his sudden, inexplicable irritation that shut her out like a pestering fly—the quick harshness, springing up in place of tenderness. She swallowed a lump in her throat. For a little while, tonight, she'd thought . . .

There was obviously something in her manner that rubbed a man the wrong way. Perhaps a man without the internal struggles that James and Ben faced wouldn't be so quick to shut her out. After all, how could a man share a war with a woman?

She glanced at Ben and her heart twisted painfully. His face was milk white. He'd leaned his head against the back of the couch and covered his eyes with one forearm. Only a few minutes ago, she had been wrapped in his embrace, feeling protected and loved and womanly. Now he would rebuff her if she tried to touch him.

She had to admit that was what she wanted to do. She wanted to stroke his brow, help him to get com-fortable, bring a pillow for his head, serve him a heal-ing cup of tea. She wanted to play a soothing melody on her guitar until he fell asleep. But she knew he wouldn't let her, not any more than James ever had.

She didn't understand it—not at all. With a reso-lute squaring of her shoulders, she promised herself that she wouldn't be hurt by this kind of situation.

A knock sounded at the door and Ben answered it before Heather had even risen. A thin, bespectacled Indian stood on the porch. "You ready?"

Ben nodded. "Give me a minute."

Heather folded her arms and in unconscious defensiveness, raised her chin slightly. She didn't cross the room.

At least he had the grace to look ashamed. "I'm sorry about tonight, Heather." His voice still carried harsh undertones.

"Don't worry about it."

He tsked softly and touched an eyebrow with one finger. "I know from experience that I'm not going to be in any shape to make conversation until I get some rest.

"You could see me out," he said quietly, when Heather didn't respond.

She sighed and left her post by the stove to walk toward the door. "Thank you, Mr. Shaw." She couldn't help the edge of sarcasm that shaded her words. "I had a lovely time."

He reached out and took her hand. The violent trembling was back in his fingers and for a fleeting second, Heather was moved to sympathy once again. Then she drew her hand away.

He closed his eyes as he paused, then swept them open to pin Heather where she stood. "I'm sorry," he repeated. "Good night."

"Good night."

Heather closed the door firmly behind him, fighting the unexpected disappointment she felt at his leaving.

Chapter Seven

Hours later, Heather lay in her bed in the darkness, staring at the ceiling. Every five minutes, her brain played back a full-color film of the entire evening from the moment Ben had appeared at her dressing-room door. It was fast forward for the scenes at the theater and through the party, up until the moment they danced palm to palm in Mike's candlelit living room. The film slowed down to illustrate Heather's easy response to the charismatic Ben Shaw, then sped through the car-drive home. It slowed again for the bedroom scene.

The film had played three dozen times already, but Heather couldn't seem to stop it. Over and over and over again, she saw herself reaching up to the shoulders of her gown and letting it fall away from her. The memory now created a mortified strangling in her throat, a weight of shame in her chest. In her entire life, even with James, she'd never behaved so *wantonly*. The word was old-fashioned, but it fit. And though Ben, like any man, had responded, she doubted he thought much of her now.

Her face burned and she squeezed her eyes tightly against the scene replaying itself again. All he'd done was kiss her, tease her, play with her—a normal reaction to her invitation to her bedroom. Had she subconsciously wished to tempt him into making love with her?

He'd wanted to. She didn't really know why he'd stopped, but she knew it had taken much effort on his part to pull away from her. When she'd been changing for their late supper, she'd thought his control a kindness, a chance to let her grow more accustomed to the idea of their becoming lovers. As she'd dressed, her skin tingling with the lingering impression of his lips and hands upon her, she'd looked forward to the rest of the evening.

Again the film had slowed, to show Ben with a stricken expression on his face, his hand on the doorknob of the workroom, and a ghastly gray tone in his skin. She'd called out to him in fear, knowing it was a seizure, and he'd slipped to the floor—not unconscious, but something far more terrifying. All manner of myths and facts about seizures had flown in and out of her mind. In the end, she'd done nothing except kneel at his side as he stared sightlessly into the hall.

Then he'd turned on her, become snarly and irritable, like a wounded animal. *Like James.* In each man, the swift mood changes meant they were in pain, but Heather had lived too long under the threat of that biting ugliness to chance facing it again. Although a deep hunger stirred within her at Ben Shaw's touch, she knew she couldn't see him again. She was infatuated with his gentleness and the sweet mystery of him, and he'd undeniably awakened something sexual within her; but she realized she couldn't face the instability she'd experienced with James—not ever again.

He called the next morning, as Heather had supposed he would. She was braced for it and answered the phone with a carefully cool "Hello?"

His voice, with its softly blurred consonants, nearly shattered her reserve right at the outset. "Heather. I'm really sorry about last night."

"I already told you that no apology is necessary."

"Oh, hell. Drop the chilly bit, would you? I acted like a jackass."

She wavered, the movie reel slipping past her mind's eye in a flurry. When it paused at the moment of their palms touching in Mike's house, a wash of new desire for him almost wiped away her decision. Then she remembered him snapping at her, shoving their date aside in hasty disregard for her feelings, and she straightened. "No big deal," she said.

"Will you let me make it up to you?"

"I don't think so. I'm really not interested in dating right now."

A pause rife with doubt traveled over the line. Heather thought of his lips on the vulnerable flesh of her lower neck and swallowed. "Heather." He sighed.

She couldn't answer for a moment, and he saved her the effort. His voice was suddenly brisk and distant, a sound that sent a crush of disappointment through her middle. "All right. You know where to find me."

The line went dead. Heather hung up slowly. He wouldn't fight for the second chance, then. So that was the end of that. The realization brought no relief, but she hadn't expected relief; she would rather suffer this little pain now, than much more, later.

When she arrived at the theater for the Saturday-night performance, another white box had been delivered, a box that weighed more than something its size should have. Heather considered sending it back, but back where? To the messenger whom no one knew? She opened the box to find a bracelet of the same cast silver as her ring and necklace, the huge tree of her necklace forming its center, with lifelike elves dancing in a circle around her wrist. Around her wrist, that is, if she put it on, which she did not. Nor did she wear the necklace or ring.

As she walked onstage for the performance, the first face she saw was Ben's. He was seated in the front row, in the seat closest to where Heather would play. To-night he wore a crisp suit, elegantly tailored, with a cream-colored silk shirt and an understated dark tie. In spite of the hair curling around his collar, he looked like an ad for some line of expensive clothing, with his square chin and broad shoulders hinting a masculine power balanced by the gentleness of his softly fringed eyes. There was no humor on his features as their eyes met, only a penetrating intensity Heather found daunting. Her body rippled with a strange awareness of his crackling sexuality, and she wondered breath-lessly as she sat down if every woman in the room could feel it.

She didn't glance at him at all throughout the per-formance, and when she looked up at the end, he was gone.

Apprehensively she headed for her dressing room, afraid to find him there, afraid she would not. Only silence greeted her, the undisturbed clutter of her street clothes scattered on the dressing table. A little pinch of disappointment touched her chest.

Mike joined her at the door. "I saw your sweetie in the audience," he said cheerily. "Are you seeing him tonight?"

Heather didn't look at him. She shook her head as she moved into the room.

"Why don't you come over for a late supper with us, then?"

"I don't know. Maybe."

Mike stepped into the room, frowning. "What is it?"

Heather moistened her lips. "I told him I didn't want to see him again."

"Oh, Heather." Mike sighed deeply. "Come here, baby." He held her in a gently rocking hug for a long moment, a wordless gesture of comfort. "Do you want to tell me about it?"

"I don't know. I don't think so, right now." She looked at him. "I guess I have to work it out on my own."

He nodded and released her. "Well, you just call me if your big brother can do anything, okay?"

She smiled halfheartedly. "Thanks."

When he had left her alone, Heather sank down into the chair in front of her mirror. The yards of velvet in her skirt soughed around her ankles. Make up your mind, Heather, she said to herself. Do you want him or not?

There was no question about the wanting, really. Only about the suitability of it—for both of them. When she thought with her brain, she knew what she had to do. She wouldn't let emotions cloud her thinking. With lips pressed together in resolve, she called Rose to help her to change her clothes.

But she hadn't reckoned on a man like Ben.

Every night, she emerged onstage to see him sitting in the same spot at the edge of the stage, his eyes burning into her as she walked to her seat. Every night she was as mesmerized by his appearance as she'd been the night before, and every night she ignored him and went back to her room.

He never followed her, never phoned, never attempted to whisper something to her as she played through the intermission. Nevertheless she could feel him watching her with an unwavering absorption.

By Tuesday, she had begun to dream of him at night—dreams filled with a kind of passion she'd never imagined she would feel for anyone, dreams that she would never have described aloud to another soul, dreams that made her face flush when they stole upon her in the morning; dreams that began to build a tense anticipation within her, an anticipation she had no means of controlling.

She didn't know when Ben would be at the theater again, but she wondered how she could possibly stand up to his physical presence when he did.

Outside Ben's window on Friday afternoon, a sharp wind rattled the pines, tossing branches at the glass, and the sky promised snow. The first real snow of the year—at least in Colorado, he thought, remembering the Kansas storm that had stalled the train.

Ordinarily, Ben anticipated the first snow on his ranch with high pleasure, but this afternoon his gaze wasn't fixed on the sky. Nor did he hear the hum of his electric typewriter as it waited for another word to be picked out in his slow manner. The last word had been typed ten minutes before, despite the fact that he'd paused midsentence.

He kept imagining Heather's face that night at her house. The wounded expression in her eyes seemed to show that she'd expected him to act as he had.

Suddenly the image became too much for Ben to stand. "John! Bring me something to eat."

"Yes, Mr. Shaw. Coming, Mr. Shaw," John replied, in a slow drawl dripping with sarcasm.

Ben lit a cigarette and clicked off the typewriter. The answer to this puzzle lay with James—or more specifically, with his suicide.

Ben remembered James only vaguely as the younger brother of one of his friends. In high school, he'd been quiet, serious. He'd rarely dated and had often gone to church two or three times a week—a habit that had earned him considerable ribbing from his older brother and his friends.

While Ben was being patched back together, James had been drafted and shipped out to Vietnam. Ben remembered thinking at the time it was a terrible place for a man with any kind of faith, but James had surprised everyone.

The story had come to Ben a couple of years later, from Mike. Though James had been reticent about the whole experience, Mike had pieced together enough about the battle to know that James probably ought to have received a more distinguished medal for bravery than the Purple Heart awarded to anyone wounded in battle.

The war had been nearly over by then, had become an embarrassment to the country, and everyone had been trying hard to forget it. Ben stubbed out his cigarette, exhaling on a sigh. Including me, he thought. When the news of James's suicide had appeared, Ben had wished he'd been a little more thoughtful, that he'd gone by to see James, or something. The wish was unrealistic, given the distant relationship between the two men, but the tragedy had upset him.

Now he wondered how Heather fit into the puzzle. What had made her feel responsible? What had James been like after the war?

John came in with a pitcher of lime Kool-Aid and a sandwich. Ben looked at them and realized he had no appetite whatsoever. "You hungry?"

The thick black glasses reflected the opaque light of the gathering storm as John shook his head. "I already ate."

"I'm grouchy enough for both of us, Rodriguez."

"Yep."

"Let's go to town." Mike would have the answers Ben sought, he decided, as he stood and stretched. "You can have the night off to see your—what's her name?"

"Elena."

"That's the one. Elena of the sultry eyes." He wiggled his nose in consideration. "I hope you don't plan on getting serious about somebody."

John shrugged. "It ain't me cryin' in my Kool-Aid."

Thursday had been a disaster, and so far, Friday had been worse, Heather thought, as she struggled with her makeup for the last performance of *Twelfth Night*. She'd smeared eyeliner halfway down one cheek and dotted mascara all over one eyebrow, then dipped lipstick over her entire chin. Needless to say, her hands had developed a slight tremor.

Last night, after an entire week of her seeing Ben's face in the audience, he hadn't appeared. Heather had gone home feeling deflated and uncertain—though her dreams had shown no uncertainty. They'd been all too vivid for Heather's comfort, and she wondered for the thirtieth time what had gotten into her.

As she slipped into her stockings, a knock sounded at the door. Before Heather had gathered herself together to open it, she'd torn a hole in the delicate nylons, upset a bottle of perfume on the vanity and nearly knocked over her chair. Her heart completely forgot the rhythm it had been repeating thousands of times every day from birth and tripped into something unrecognizable. At the door she paused, her palms as wet as grass at dawn, her mind a whirl of possibilities. "Who is it?" she called.

"Tom, from your Thursday-morning class?" He ended on a question, as if he weren't sure he would be welcome.

Heather let go of her breath and opened the door. "Hello. I'm so glad to see you," she greeted sincerely.

Tom wore a poorly made brown suit sans tie, and the telltale color of his shyness crept up his cheeks toward his eyes. In his hand he held a single pink rose. "I just came by to wish you luck," he said.

Heather was moved by his discomfort. Why did he always feel as if he didn't belong? "Come in. I'm almost finished." She turned away from the door and sat at the vanity to put on her shoes. In the hallway, the excited voices of the company floated down airily. "Did you have a chance to look over the piece I brought you yesterday?"

"I did, Heather." The color receded from his face and he approached her eagerly. "I'm here tonight to tell you that I think you should play it."

She paused, her hand at her ankle. "I think you've been talking to my brother-in-law."

"You're right," he admitted. "But I'm not stupid. You have something good with that steel-mill thing. I picked it out last night—not real good, you know— but enough to understand a little bit of what you did." He sat on a stool near her, his eyes very serious. "What are you doing *here*?"

Heather didn't know what to say. She cocked her head for a moment in indecision. If her instinct was right about Tom, he was a latent genius on the guitar, which meant his ear was acute. She frowned. "It isn't really quite finished," she said.

"Yes, it is, Heather. You have to stop polishing it and let it go." He moistened his lips and leaned forward. "Play it tonight."

"It's too long for intermission," she protested.

"Mike wants you to play it afterward—a kind of special addition or something." He paused, a smile coming to his mouth. "If you'll do it, I'll go to the university Monday morning and talk to the guy you wanted me to see."

Still, Heather hesitated. Then, all at once, she capitulated with a grin. "You have a deal." What did she have to lose, after all? No one had to know the piece was something she'd worked on for years, that it was a deeply personal observation of the cycle of the mill. Tom was talented enough that she owed him any chance she could give him to get involved with good teachers.

"Great." He stood and stuck out a hand.

Heather stood to accept it. "Keep at it and maybe we can play a duet in a week or two."

He nodded. "Terrific!" he responded, and left her to practice.

By the time she had to take her place on stage, Heather was considerably calmer. There had been no word from Ben and she had to believe that he'd given up. The knowledge brought disappointment, but it eased the burden of mingled fear and hunger she felt toward him.

Even her unresolved feelings for Ben took a back seat to her anticipation at debuting the steel-mill piece. In her dressing room, she'd run through the sonata, suspended in a sense of disbelief as the familiar notes emerged, with all their attendant memories. She couldn't quite believe she'd actually agreed to perform it.

The play itself passed in a whirl of anticipation. When the actors took their bows, a strange calm invaded Heather—a certainty that it was the right moment, the right circumstance, the right *everything*, to debut the piece. She didn't even feel any alarm when Mike ran out onstage as the actors exited.

"Ladies and gentlemen, as I promised before the play, we have a special treat for you tonight." He gestured toward Heather with an open palm. "I have the great pleasure of announcing that Heather Scarborough, our esteemed guitarist, will debut a composition this evening. It is untitled, but I like to think of it as a tribute to the steel mill and its cycles. I know you'll enjoy it."

Still moving in the narrowed world of fatalism, Heather bent her head over her guitar, paused, then began the sonata. As she played, her imagination furnished the images that the music had captured in her mind, the bits of legend and lore that had so fascinated her upon coming to Pueblo—the traffic along the side streets leading to the mill, the laundry black with smoke, the hearty men who braved the mill for the money and benefits that lifted an entire city of immigrants from Eastern Europe, Italy and Mexico to standards of living they'd never even dreamed of. The first movement depicted the rich satisfaction and good times of those days.

Then came the lay-offs and the false hopes of temporary unemployment fading into the grim reality of wives returning to work. The second movement captured the sorrowful days of a collapsing economy, of more houses up for sale than the market could handle, of the once-proud men, uneducated to any other form of work, struggling first with self-esteem, then despair, and finally, a humble acceptance of community programs designed to train them to do something new.

The third movement exuded the poignance of broken dreams forged with new ones—the children going away but eventually returning to a city changing, expanding, growing; a city maturing beyond the "adolescence" of industrialization.

As she played, Heather was swept into a realization that the piece worked. A kind of exhilaration flooded through her, and her throat tightened with triumph. Her ears, her heart, every fiber of her artistic being told her the notes conjured up the visions she had meant them to; that anyone who understood the cycle of the city would hear it in her work. As she repeated the theme of each movement at the end, her heart swelled unbearably.

The last notes were the ones inspired the night James died: the steel mill under cover of heavy clouds, the stacks black and strangely graceful against the pinkish sky, standing in mute reminder of all the city had been, and in a curious way, all it had the potential to become.

The music died away in a silent auditorium and Heather raised her head. The audience sat utterly still, and for a brief second, a fear that she'd been alone in her vision seized her. Then she saw tears in the eyes of a man—*a man*—in one of the front rows and she stood, guitar at her side, to the applause that began to rumble from the back and sides of the theater, a thunderous clapping that rolled around and embraced her. Cheers whooped down and the audience, as one person, leaped to its feet. It went on and on and on, and Heather stood in the center, suddenly sure that she was exactly where she was meant to be.

With every molecule of her body thrumming with wild energy, she curtsied deeply, raised her guitar in salute, and left the stage. Never in her entire life had she felt as good as she did in those moments, with the applause ringing in her ears and the tears of one man engraved in her memory. Even if it never came again, the time to play that piece had been right tonight.

The roaring of the audience still echoed in her ears as the cast and crew milled into the corridor below the seats and stage after the play. Heather managed to make her way through the throng, amid claps and congratulations, hearing none of it, aware of a desire to be alone for one moment to relish the wonderful thing that had happened.

She wasn't to get her wish. Tom waited at her door. He hugged her spontaneously, then set her down with a flourish. "I'll see a teacher every day for a month for you, lady. That was fantastic."

Heather laughed, a remarkably throaty sound, a richer laugh than she ever remembered emerging from her mouth before. "I owe it to you, because I never would have played it on my own."

He smiled and saluted her. "I just wanted to congratulate you."

"Come by Monday after you talk to the instructor and let me know how it went."

"Here?"

"No. Mondays I'm off. Ask Mike to bring you by the house, or tell you where it is."

"Okay."

She opened her door, about to move inside, when another voice stopped her. "Miss Scarborough?"

The voice belonged to a middle-aged man in evening dress. "My name is George Wilkes," he announced, extending his hand. "I'm about to open a new evening club here. I wonder if I might talk to you for a moment?"

Heather shook her head. "Yes. Come in."

"How would you like a job, Miss Scarborough? Playing just the way you have all week in my new club."

"Me?"

The man grinned. "You," he said firmly. "You play quite beautifully, and that tribute tonight was really something."

"Thank you."

"I won't press you for an answer tonight. I'm opening on Union Avenue next week. It's a nice place, a little different than anything we've had here before. You'd make a nice addition." He withdrew a business card and pressed it into her hand. "Give me a call in a day or two."

"I don't have to think about it, Mr. Wilkes. I need the money."

He smiled. "Good. Call me the first part of next week and we'll set it up." He named a figure that would nearly triple her monthly income. "Does that sound fair?"

"Very."

"I'll talk to you next week, then."

Rose had barely helped her change into a pair of jeans and a warm sweater before a press of cast and crew crowded into her room. Heather met them happily, accepting kisses and hugs of congratulations. Mike's wife, Ellen, embraced her warmly. "Where's that good-lookin' man you had with you last week?"

"I don't know," Heather said, her voice remarkably even.

Ellen lifted an eyebrow archly. "If I weren't married—" she said, and laughed as Mike grabbed her from behind.

"If you weren't married, what, wench?" He dipped her backward into a kiss and Ellen laughed again, slapping at him playfully.

"I'd run away with that handsome cowboy."

"And leave me to my gorgeous sister-in-law? Ha! You'd die of jealousy first."

Heather watched their teasing with envy. After seventeen years of marriage and uncountable tests, they still loved one another; and whatever either of them said, they would remain married—Heather was sure of it. A spasm of loneliness touched her. No matter how well her work went, no matter what came of this triumph tonight, the fact was, she had no one to share it with.

A murmur rustled through the gathered well-wishers and Heather glanced toward the door. Very slowly she turned, a powerful sense of destiny touching her again. For there, filling the doorway, was Ben. The room dropped away. There was no sound, no sensation— only her eyes, fixed on Ben, were capable of reaction.

This, too, was part of this night, she thought; his eyes molten with a hunger he didn't bother to mask. Heather felt her tension fade as she drank in his appearance, his relaxed stance, the ease of his coat thrown over one strong shoulder, his hair richly gleaming, falling over his forehead and curling around his neck. He didn't move for the longest time, and then, with deliberate, unhurried movements, he headed through the crowd toward her.

Heather was frozen in place, her gaze riveted upon him, the subject of all her dreams and long-hidden yearnings. Suddenly she didn't care about James, about the play, about the job she'd been offered. Nothing mattered except Ben's slow advance across the room. He paused inches away from her, and Heather's universe was filled with his lean face and beautiful eyes before he swept her into an engulfing embrace. Heather threw her arms around his neck and pressed into his long length, a sense of relief uppermost as his arms encircled her. "I missed you, Heather," he whispered. His mustache brushed her neck.

She said nothing at all, smelling his foresty aftershave and the whisper of leather. Against her breasts, his chest was solid and reassuring and male; under her fingers, his shoulder muscles stretched and his hair brushed her wrist. Her cheek rested on his shoulder. "I thought, last night, that you might have given up," she breathed.

"I did. But I couldn't sleep." He eased his hold to look at her. "I had to see you one more time, anyway."

"I'm glad."

"Can I kidnap you?"

Heather smiled. "As long as you do it right now."

"I've got a cab right outside." He tangled his fingers in hers. "Let's go."

Heather followed him through the crowd, unaware of the approving glances that rested upon them.

Outside, Ben stopped and pressed her into the wall. The cold night swirled around them and Heather shivered. Ben lowered his head to take her lips, his mouth a heated island in the frigid night. His tongue touched hers and Heather sighed. All of her dreams came back to her—dreams full of his lips and eyes and hands—and the simmering anticipation swelled into existence again.

Ben pulled away with reluctance. "I'll tell you right now, I'm obsessed with you," he said softly. "There's just no other word for it." He cupped her cheek in his palm. "I'm going to take you home with me, but I want you to know there's no pressure. We don't have to make love. I just want to be with you. I want to get to know you."

Heather nodded.

"Come on, let's get that cab."

The significance of his words sank in. "Ben, we can't take a cab all the way to Beulah. I have my car. Let's drive that."

He shook his head, and the old familiar mischief was back in his eyes. "Nope, I want your attention all to myself."

For a moment Heather wondered if it was wise to go off with him and have no escape route open to her. Right now, she felt fevered and unlike herself, high on the triumph of her success and on being with Ben again after so many long days. Would she feel the same way in a few hours?

He seemed to sense her hesitation and tugged her hand lightly. "I'm not Bluebeard," he assured her. "I promise."

A gust of wind blasted the small cement platform on which they stood. "Okay. I trust you."

They ran for the waiting cab. "Beulah," Ben told the driver.

"No problem, buddy." He glanced in the rearview mirror oddly. "Don't I know you, man?"

"Where'd you go to school?"

"Central. Would have been the class of '69, but I didn't make it that far."

"Joe Riley."

"Yeah. Who are you?"

"Ben Shaw."

"I remember. The rodeo rider. You're a veteran, too, eh?"

Ben looped his arm around Heather, pulling her close to him. "Yeah," he answered, his chin in her hair. Heather found her hand on his stomach, and almost unconsciously began to move her palm in a circle, gauging tensity of skin and muscles and bone below the striped maroon shirt, as wonderingly delighted by the sensation as a child exploring her mother's face. She relaxed into him, her ear on his chest. When he spoke to the driver, his voice rumbled into her, vibratory and deep. At her crown, she could feel his jaw moving.

After a time, the mood of easy comfort between them richened into something deliciously unhurried and yet sensual. Heather found herself shifting to explore the line of his chest, felt the tiny nipple stiffen as she passed over it, felt the heat of his skin as she moved her fingers to his face, felt the soft bristles of his magnificent mustache as she slid her hand over his cheek. She continued the lazy exploration with her eyes closed, touching his ear, his temple, his scalp below the cool weight of his hair.

Ben's conversation trailed away and the driver turned up his music as they headed out of town on a straight highway surrounded by open prairie. Ben kissed her forehead and both of her eyes, her nose and each cheekbone, her jaw and chin and mouth—all lightly, in a whisper of heat and hair and full lips. He slipped his hands away from her neck and over her arms, her sides, her waist, easing up almost unbearably towards her breasts, always stopping just below or alongside. Heather felt an alarming surge of sexual awareness engulfing her, a tide that swept all reason away with it, a tide that had nothing to do with reality, only these stolen moments in a dark cab.

He kissed her neck teasingly, and Heather laughed, again with that throatily rich sound she'd never heard from herself before this night. Ben tightened his fingers on her sides almost painfully and he ceased his exploration. Heather's laughter died at the expression in his eyes, a startled and passionate penetration that surpassed any playfulness she'd been feeling and kindled an explosion of yearning within her. She thrilled to the sudden, fierce crush of his mouth upon hers, the hard thrust of his tongue, the nip of his teeth and his strangling grip. It was as if he wanted to inhale her, and Heather welcomed it with explorations of her own. She pressed into him and tilted her head to more readily accommodate his kiss, tangling her fingers in his hair in the process. Never had a man

created this kind of emotion in her. Not even James
had stirred anything remotely close to what she now
felt in Ben's arms, under the power of his kiss. She felt
both needed and hungry, soothed and stimulated,
wildly infatuated and deeply cherished. She didn't
analyze or worry, and that, too, was new. She abandoned herself to him and the ravenous nature of his
embrace.

Where they would have ended up was beyond spec-
ulation. But suddenly the driver cleared his throat, a
sound so shattering that Heather and Ben broke apart
like fighting cats doused with water. "I need to know
where to take you now. We're in Beulah."

Ben sighed and pulled Heather next to him. As he
gave directions, he held her tightly. Heather was
grateful for the cover of darkness. What had gotten
into her? Running off into the night with a man she'd
met less than two weeks before, tumbling into his
arms—practically making love in the cab, for heav-
en's sake.

Yet, as she leaned into that very same man, her lips
burning and tingling with the impression of his forceful mouth, she still wanted him. Wanted him more
than she'd ever wanted anything in her life.

Passion had always been something she'd read
about, not something that was made for real life. With
James, she'd enjoyed making love, had enjoyed his
touch and his kisses. But this was so different, she
couldn't even think of an analogy for it—it was like
wanting fresh collard greens in the dead of winter or

wanting to devour an entire pound of caviar, no matter how sick she would be afterward. It was like the compulsion of people who eat clay to satisfy their craving for iron.

It was completely beyond her, out of her control. And she had no idea what to do about it.

Chapter Eight

Ben's house sat nestled in a cove of pine trees. As he paid the driver, Heather hid her discomfort by studying the broad front porch. How she would get through the next ten minutes, she had no idea.

"Come on, darlin', it's cold out here," Ben said, taking her arm. She followed him up the steps of the veranda and waited while he fit the key into the lock. To her left, a huge tree shielded the porch from the hard, westerly sunlight that would otherwise bake the front of the house on summer evenings; and to the east stretched the low, rolling prairie lands they had traveled over from Pueblo. Behind the home rose the Rockies. The air smelled freshly washed, imbued with the lightness only mountain air carries, and by a note of wood smoke mingled with pine and earth.

Ben opened the door and moved aside to let Heather in. At that instant a huge creature romped through the opening onto the porch, nearly knocking Heather down. She gave a little cry and moved aside hastily. A sweeping tail slapped into her jeans-clad legs, and the click of nails against wood skittered at her feet. Heather giggled and reached out to touch the dog's back. "What a big animal! What is it?"

"A dog, sort of."

Heather laughed. "I know that, silly. What kind of dog?"

"Newfoundland and Saint Bernard. And I'd be careful about being friendly if I were you. He thinks he's a lapdog."

The dog licked Heather's hand and she bent to hug him. It was like embracing a bear. He made a loving sound in his throat and lay his chin on her shoulder. "He's sweet."

"You'll change your mind in an hour when he tries to set two hundred pounds on your lap." There was a hint of indulgence to his words. "Get up, Woody."

The dog complied and Heather rose, realizing that in some magical way, Ben's pet had broken the tension created by the interrupted passion in the cab. She smiled. "I'm starved. Do you have anything to eat?"

Ben relaxed visibly and touched the side of his nose in the gesture she'd come to think of when he was away from her. "Lots. Come on in."

At the door, Woody tried to squeeze between the couple and nearly overturned both humans. "Woody," Ben warned, "get the heck out the way, boy. I'll get you something to eat, too."

Heather paused just inside the threshold, feeling a catch in her throat. It was utterly, completely different from her own, staid living room. Here, rubbed and varnished light pine covered the walls, and a series of woven rugs in muted, Southwestern colors dotted the wooden floor. At one corner, two large multipaned windows opened to a view of pines and sky. The furniture was low, upholstered in shades of blue and lavender and clay, and unadorned small tables rested nearby the chairs and couches. Along the walls, shelves held collections of an odd variety of items. One group caught Heather's eye and she crossed the room to take a better look. "What are these?" she asked, picking up an old bottle with a clear brownish liquid inside. The label read Sloan's Linament and showed a line drawing of a man in an old-fashioned suit.

Ben had gone ahead to the kitchen and he appeared in the doorway, grinning. "Patent medicine. I found that one, believe it or not, in a ghost town when I was a kid."

"I'll bet a few of them really pack a punch," she said, and put it down. A little farther away sat a cluster of carved ivory figurines. "And these?" she asked.

"Mementos."

She looked at him. "Of Vietnam?"

He nodded.

"I wouldn't think you'd want reminders."

Ben crossed the room and picked out one of the carvings, an exquisitely detailed elephant. "Nothing's ever all bad, Heather," he said. "When I get tempted to feel sorry for myself, these help me to remember some of the things I learned there."

"Like what?"

He put the figurine in her palm and closed her fingers over it. When he spoke again, his eyes shone with a soft, pulsing energy. "Like there must be something good about a culture that invented a word for 'beautiful beyond description.'"

Heather dropped her gaze, feeling the trunk of the elephant against her fingers. At that moment, her stomach growled loudly. "I think I'd better see what your kitchen has before I start eating these," she warned playfully. "Sorry about that."

He laughed. "Perfectly natural."

The kitchen, too, was beautiful, showing foresight and planning. "Did you build this house?" Heather asked, sweeping a hand over the smooth counter of the center island. Above it hung a variety of cast-iron pots and spatulas, whisks and spoons.

"No, I bought it from an old couple who used it as a summer home." He glanced up from his survey of the refrigerator shelves. "Great kitchen, isn't it?"

"It is," she agreed. "Are you a good cook?"

The warm dark eyes glinted. "Pretty good. Are you?"

"Absolutely terrible. I hate cooking with all my heart."

"That's why you eat all that good-for-you food." As if to push the point home, he pulled out a pitcher of red Kool-Aid. "Want some?"

Heather raised her eyebrows. "Do you have anything else?"

"Sure. Tea, coffee, water. Probably some pop— John likes pop." He swiveled toward a bank of cupboards on the wall and drew out a glass. As he poured the jewel-colored liquid he asked, "How long as it been since you had a glass of Kool-Aid?"

She smiled. "Oh, a hundred years or so."

"Try some."

She inclined her head.

"Come on. One sip." His eyes glittered in their frame of laugh lines and he leaned casually against the counter, his long legs emphasized by the easy cross of his ankles. He'd removed his coat and tie, and at the collar of his shirt, a triangle of golden skin showed. His inky hair had been mussed in the car and curled around his ears and neck in a boyish way. Heather found herself moving toward him and accepting the glass.

She really had forgotten how wonderful cold, cold Kool-Aid could taste; how well it soothed dry throat tissues and how it landed with a delicious, icy splash in her stomach. "Not bad," she said, and drank again. "Black cherry."

With a grin, Ben poured himself another glass. "You keep that one. And let's see what else I can rustle up around here."

He pulled tomatoes, celery and a green pepper from the crisper and gave them to Heather. "You can slice stuff, can't you?"

"I'm not *that* bad in the kitchen."

"Glad to hear it." He dipped back into the fridge and pulled out a banana pudding, obviously fresh, made of layers of cookies and topped with floating circles of banana. Heather groaned softly. "I haven't had banana pudding in a hundred years, either."

"You probably haven't had a lot of things you should have had in a long time," Ben commented. Since Heather couldn't tell if there was a double meaning implied, she let it slide, and went on slicing vegetables.

The spread he assembled on a tray included the pudding and the vegetables, a pair of apples, crackers, and a pepperoni. "Come on, let's eat in the other room where we can turn on some music."

Ben lit a fire and turned on the stereo. "Go ahead. I'm going to take these boots off."

The fire, expertly built, began to flicker as the kindling took hold, and soft bluegrass music drifted from the stereo. Heather kicked off her own shoes and sat down on the rug before the fire. By the time Ben returned, she'd dug into her second helping of pudding, completely ignoring the fresh vegetables that would, under any other circumstances, have been her only choice. Vegetables and water.

"This is wonderful, Ben," she said as he sat down. "Thank you."

"I'm glad you like it. Is this the kind of food your mother made?"

"Yes. Banana pudding on Sundays, to top off the pot roast. Meat loaf on Mondays, chicken Tuesdays, pork chops on Wednesdays..." She shifted, remembering. "I hated dinner."

Ben laughed. "I guess you would. Why did she always make the same thing?"

"That's how they did things. My father came home from work at five on the dot, drank a Scotch and water and dozed while my mother set the table. We ate at five-thirty, went to bed right after the seven o'clock news." Heather savored the taste of a vanilla wafer before continuing. "It's still like that in my mother's house. I get claustrophobic every time I go there."

Ben sliced the pepperoni. "My folks weren't like that at all." He laughed a little. "Too many of us, for one thing, and everybody busy all the time—this kid here, that kid there. My mom used to make a lot of soups and stews and stuff that you could eat on the run. And she baked a lot."

"How many of you?"

"Seven. Three girls and four boys."

"Where are you? Oldest, youngest, what?"

"Exactly the middle." His mustache wiggled under his grin. "That's why I'm such a loving fellow."

Heather considered him. "All that family doesn't hurt. It must have been wonderful to be surrounded by so much noise and energy. I hated being an only child."

Woody joined them, laying his head on Heather's lap. The conversation turned to pets and childhood escapades. Heather found herself telling him about her sixth-grade best friend and the way they'd folded their notes to one another, about her love of the Mississippi River and the history of her home city, about books she'd read in high-school English class and her suspension from school for smoking in the washroom.

She relaxed in a way she'd forgotten she could. With her stomach full, she leaned back on one arm and let the fire toast one side of her body and then the other. The tray of food was pushed out of the way, and Ben made cups of tea.

In turn, he shared stories of his life on a ranch amid noise and confusion and love; told her about each of his siblings—all married and settled in careers or marriages all over the western United States. His parents had moved to Arizona with one of their daughters after the cold winters became too much for his mother's arthritis.

When their tea had grown cold, Heather heard herself ask, "What about Vietnam? How did you end up going?"

He sighed softly, and in a gesture Heather knew was unconscious, grabbed his bad ankle. "I just went. It seemed like the thing to do at the time."

"Do you ever regret it?"

His gaze was serious. "I try not to regret anything I've ever done." He looked at the fire. The light sharpened the straight bridge of his nose and set his mustache alight with red tints. "I think everybody does the best they can. Most people." He looked at her. "Good people."

"I guess so."

He stood. "I know so." He held out a hand to help Heather up and pulled her into a soft embrace. In the flickering light his eyes were gentle, and Heather wondered, as she had on the train, what made a face seem kind. For if there had ever been a kind face, he had one. There was no trace of weakness—the chin and jaw and the firm set of the mouth were too determined for that—but something made it gentle nonetheless. He bent to kiss her lightly. "I'm going to send you to bed now, Titania. I really meant it when I said I wanted to get to know you." He grinned ruefully. "Not that I wouldn't like a little different end to the evening, but you still aren't ready for that." He kissed her again. "I have lots of time."

The touch of his lips, however gentle, hinted at a sensuality held in check by sheer force of will; and Heather felt a like response. She wasn't sure whether to feel relieved or disappointed when he firmly set her away from him and led her to a bedroom.

It was his room, as it turned out, and he assured her with a grin that the sheets were clean before he turned to go. "See you in the morning, Heather."

She stopped him. "Thank you, Ben. I've had a really wonderful time tonight."

He grinned and left her to what he hoped would be a good night's sleep.

As the fire burned to embers in the dark living room, Ben smoked meditatively, far too aware of the woman in the other room to sleep. All evening he had wrestled with himself. His emotions and heart had urged him to make love with her, knowing she wouldn't resist. It was his head that had insisted she wasn't ready; that if they made love, she would run.

All evening, he'd watched the fire play over her pale yellow braid and leap in her eyes, had admired the lean curve of her hips and slender shoulders. She had a mobile mouth, a mouth that expressed every thought in her mind with frowns and pouts and tiny tremblings, or smiles and quirky corners; a mouth as sweet and tender as June strawberries.

He took a long drag from the cigarette and exhaled slowly. He hadn't been exaggerating when he'd told her he was obsessed. No woman had ever crawled under his skin to lay her palm on his soul in this way. The night he'd met her, he'd got a full-blown idea for a new novel and the damn thing was almost completely written. Two weeks. He usually labored several months, at least, to get the scenes and words and people right.

Not this time. He was up at the crack of dawn unable to resist the lure of the typewriter, after nights of characters whispering to him while he slept. He wrote for hours without pause and finished the day about suppertime, as exhilarated as he had ever been on the back of a bucking stallion.

The novel's concept was a complete departure for him, as well. It was still the Old West, but the similarity stopped there. The main character wasn't a soldier or a ranch hand or an Indian. It was a little girl, growing and observing the West as it grew—a curious and friendly little girl, a character he loved, who'd been inspired by the grown woman in the other room.

He couldn't pinpoint what it was about Heather that so caught his imagination and heart and soul. He liked women—always had—and he'd fancied himself in love a few times. But it had never been like this.

Tonight when she'd played her steel-mill piece, Ben had been riveted, seeing clearly the cycle of the mill as he'd grown up: the cocky confidence of the millworkers with their full pockets; their despair when foreign steel beat American; the bad, bad days when the state had been certain that Pueblo would dry up and blow away.

He wondered at the elusive quality of music that could capture something like emotions without using words to draw the pictures. To him, it was unfathomable that she could do it, as amazing as if she could weave spells to make it rain. The last movement of the piece told of the gathering of resources and the sturdiness of a people, proud and unbreakable, realigning their priorities and finding something else they would be good at. He'd felt a catch in his throat, a deep pride in the people of the city, a city that tended to be dismissed as backward in the cosmopolitan state of Colorado. Pueblo didn't quite fit in with the image of snowy Rockies and glittering resorts that the rest of the state wanted to portray. Like an uncle from the Old Country, Pueblo remained stubbornly set in its ways, clinging to values of home and family and marriage forever.

Heather—a woman from another city, a lonely child finding home in the lap of that kindly old uncle—had made it all seem noble with her guitar. He'd almost been overcome as he'd listened, as his pride in the city mingled with his pride for Heather.

He stubbed out his cigarette. He intended to see that she got that piece published. He wanted to see it played all over Colorado. She would have to pushed, he figured, but he'd be damned if he would let her hide that incredible light of talent under a bushel.

Comforted by the thought, he slipped down under the heavy quilt on the couch and slept as deeply as he ever had, with visions of Heather dancing in his head.

Heather awoke to a pale gray morning, and when she peeked out the window, saw thick, heavy snowflakes falling to a pristine landscape. The rich odor of percolating coffee told her Ben was up before her, and she hurried through her morning ablutions, dressing and washing her face, then freeing her hair from the braid that had mercifully kept it tangle free through the night.

Ben, hearing the noises of her stirring, called through the bathroom door, "There's a new toothbrush in the medicine cabinet."

Again she was struck by his thoughtfulness—a simple awareness of human needs beyond his own. She brushed her teeth and joined him in the warm kitchen. "Good morning."

He stood by the stove, cooking bacon. He wore a clean green corduroy shirt that pointed up the warm tones of his skin and the darkness of his hair. He smiled at her. "Mornin'. Cup of coffee?"

"Sure. I can get it."

"Allow me." He poured a mug full of the steamy brew and crossed the room to give it to her. "Gives me a chance to steal a kiss."

His lips touched hers lightly and as he pulled back, he lifted a handful of her hair in his fist to let it fall, strand by stand, back into place. "You look like an angel with all this hair."

"Thank you," she said quietly, thinking he looked rather wonderful himself.

He returned to the stove. "Do you know how to ride a horse?"

"No. I've never even been close to one, believe it or not. I've never had the chance."

"I've got two out in my barn. Are you in the mood to try something new?"

Heather shrugged, feeling uncertain. "I guess."

"I think you're the kind of person who would like horses. I know they'll like you."

"What makes you think so?" Heather asked skeptically. "I'm not known for my hardy outdoorsiness."

That elicited a grin. "You're not the namby-pamby you make yourself out to be, either. You've got plenty of heart. Horses know heart and they like it, just like big dogs do." He fished out strips of bacon and drained them on a paper towel, then opened the oven, and she glimpsed a tray of almost golden biscuits before he closed it again. "Almost done. You like scrambled eggs?"

"Sure. I'm more interested in those biscuits, however. Did you make them from scratch?"

"One of my specialties." He glanced over his shoulder at her, a twinkle sparkling in his eyes.

Heather responded with a laugh, throaty and warm, and as it emerged, she thought she was getting used to the sound. "No man ever cooked breakfast for me."

"Their loss."

He took the biscuits out and put Heather to work buttering them while he finished the eggs. A pitcher of orange juice completed the meal and they both ate like wolverines, utterly concentrating upon their food, taking little time for even the politest of conversation. Heather couldn't remember the last time a meal

had tasted so wonderful. Must be the mountain air,
she decided.

After breakfast, Ben disappeared into one of the
back rooms and returned wearing a duster—a knee-
length, split-back coat made for riding. In his hand he
carried one for Heather. "This is John's. You'll have
to roll up the sleeves, but it'll keep your legs from
freezing."

She tried it on and laughed. It fell nearly to her ankles and the shoulders dwarfed her. But she had to
admit it was warm. Ben wrapped a scarf around her
neck and gave her a cowboy hat of soft suede to wear.

The barn was a weathered old building west of the
house. It nestled against the bosom of the mountain
behind it like a small child against its mother. Inside
it smelled of animals, hay and wet wood, and Heather
breathed deeply as she waited for her eyes to adjust to
the gloom.

Ben led her to a cream-colored horse that calmly
munched some kind of grain. Heather felt herself
holding back, afraid despite her best intentions. Ben
paused. "This is Sugar. She's been my horse for a long
time." He nickered and the animal moved slowly toward them, her big nose nuzzling Ben's pockets.

Although Heather had shrunk close to Ben's side,
she noted with fascination the velvety appearance of
that nose, noticed the flare of her nostrils as Sugar
breathed. Heather reached out a hand to touch the
long nose, only to draw back in giddy terror when the
horse lifted her head.

Ben laughed low in his throat and slipped an arm around her in comfort. "Go ahead. She doesn't bite."

Heather, reassured by his confidence around the animal, tried again. This time her finger encountered the nose and found it to be as soft as it looked. She moved her fingers up and down, touching the spray of white hair mingled in with the tan between the horse's eyes, and was entranced by the warmth and size of the muzzle. Sugar endured it for a moment, then snorted. Heather jerked her hand back.

"She wants something to eat." Ben reached into his pocket and put a sugar cube in Heather's hand. "Hold it out."

She reached toward the horse with a trembling palm, giggling when Sugar's soft mouth lifted the cube.

"Would you like to ride her?"

"Boy, you don't believe in taking it easy, do you?"

"Not about horses." His eyes took on the smoldering look she'd grown to recognize and Heather swallowed at the instant response that leaped within her. If it hadn't been for his control . . . Well, he was right. As much as she wanted him, she wasn't ready.

"Okay," she heard herself agree. "I'll try."

Ben boosted her onto the horse's back. "I learned to ride bareback," he said, "and I think you get a better feel for what goes on inside a horse when you do. Just hang on to her mane. If we were going anywhere, I'd put a bridle and blanket on, but there's no way she'll go outside in this kind of weather."

Oddly, once perched on Sugar's back, Heather felt her terror slip away. The animal's back was broad and warm, the hair prickly through her jeans. The mane was thick and coarse and much softer than Heather would have imagined. When Ben began to lead her around the barn, Heather felt the horse's muscles shifting and sliding under her thighs. It gave her a powerful feeling to ride so high. "I think I might like this," she admitted.

"Good." He stopped and lifted his hands to help her down. "Let's go riding."

"I thought you said she won't go out in this weather?"

"She won't. Buffalo will." He nodded at the big black horse in the corner. "We'll ride together, just a little ways." As he spoke, he threw two wool blankets over Buffalo's huge sable back. The horse whinnied and danced sideways for a moment, then allowed himself to be bridled. Ben led him to the barn doors. "I think I'll take him out for a minute, let him get the restlessness burned off a little." He winked at Heather, then using his good leg to spring, jumped astride the great beast.

Heather watched from the barn doors as Ben walked Buffalo down a short path to an empty field. The sight of him on a horse literally stole her breath. His body took on a fluid yet tensile nature that made him seem utterly at home in a way that he never was on foot because of his limp, however much it had become a part of him. Just as his face seemed to be designed for laughing, his lean body looked made for riding. His black hair curled out from below his weathered hat, and the duster split neatly over the horse's back to cover Ben's long legs. Heavy snowflakes clung to his shoulders and arms and hat. He was beautiful on the back of his horse—a refugee from one of his novels, a proud man comfortable with the elements, ready to tangle with gunfighters or smoke a pipe with the elders of a local Indian tribe. His masculine profile showed a strong nose and full lips. He was looking off into the distance as if he could see forever. Heather felt decidedly dizzy at the sight.

When man and horse reached the field, Ben led the straining animal in circles, and when Buffalo had ceased his restless pacing, brought him back toward Heather, moving silently in the endless landscape.

As they approached, Heather felt her breath coming in shallow gasps, as if her sustenance depended not upon the air she breathed but upon filling her eyes and heart with the sight of this magnificent man. The ride had flushed his cheeks and lent a leaping excitement to his eyes. He guided the horse to Heather's side. "You ready?"

She nodded eagerly.

"Climb up on that fence and I'll get you."

She eased onto the horse behind Ben and slipped her arms around his waist. "Don't go too fast," she asked.

"I won't, honey," he assured her. "Hang on. You're going to love it."

They headed back to the field at a mellow pace and Heather, whc'd been holding on to Ben's waist for dear life, eased her grip to look around her. The heavy snowfall drifted over the trees that rose at the foot of the mountain, over the plants and shrubs that dotted the field and over Ben's house behind them, giving off a magical, mystical elegance. She stuck her tongue out to catch the ethereal snowflakes and reveled in their cold taste. Ben's scent enveloped her. The soft air swirled around her face and she thought she'd never felt more alive than she did at this moment.

"Are you okay back there?"

"I'm fine!" She leaned into the solid expanse of Ben's back and tried to sense what he meant about the muscles of the horse. Somehow, Ben seemed to move with the animal in a way that she wasn't. She closed her eyes and relaxed her body, suddenly feeling a rhythm beneath her.

Buffalo moved with sure grace over the field, and Heather felt her hair whip out behind her as a cold wind blew. As she fit her arms more snugly around Ben's waist, she reveled in the comfort of his body next to hers. "This is glorious!" she called to him.

"Best thing in the world to me."

She could understand how he'd been able to win the titles he'd claimed in high-school rodeo. Seeing him on a horse brought home the best of him, made clear the reasons he wrote the way he did, emphasized the forceful yet gentle personality.

With a start, Heather realized that her emotions had passed infatuation and gone beyond even the heady sexual awareness she felt toward him—a sexuality any woman in her right mind would experience in his presence. She didn't quite know what she felt, but her growing sensitivity to him was frightening.

The field ended at a grove of pine trees. Ben led them into it a little way and paused. "This is my chapel," he said softly. "I come here to get myself together when I'm not. I even sleep here in the summertime."

She looked around. Tall, deep green firs, pines and spruce bent their graceful arms toward the earth. The silence was as unbroken as a frozen pool and she felt the hush was like a spirit's presence. "I can see why."

"Let's get down. I want to show you something."

A surge of anticipation tightened the muscles of her belly as she slid from the horse into his arms. He took her hand and they waded through the snow to an enormous old tree, seventy feet high. The branches on the lower trunk had fallen away up to about seven feet, leaving a protected cove at the base of the trunk. Around it sprang an assortment of other greenery— pinon and spruce and a bush Heather didn't recognize.

Ben led her inside the cove of branches. Below the tree, the ground was dry and soft with years of fallen needles, and was dotted with pinecones. "It's like a little room," she said in wonder.

"Look up."

She did. Above stretched the mighty tree, thick branches hiding the sky as effectively as a roof. It was incredible, like a child's hideaway. She smiled at Ben, her fears of the moment before forgotten as he once again cast his spell over her. A tiny voice in her mind warned, *You're in over your head.* But Heather ignored it. "Can we stay here for a little while?"

He nodded, strangely sober, his eyes below his hat taking on a deep intensity. "Let me get one of the blankets from Buffalo."

He left her and Heather leaned on the tree. It smelled spicy, and the warmth of the cove surprised her. Again she looked up through the branches, peering for a glimpse of the sky. It was a mystical place, she thought; a secret, private thing. She felt gratitude toward Ben for sharing it with her.

When he returned with the blanket, Heather looked at him. Very seriously she said, "Thank you for bringing me here, Ben. It's beautiful."

His expression softened. He threw the blanket around her shoulders and drew her toward him. "It's my pleasure," he responded and kissed her lightly. His lips were cool at first, warming as the kiss lengthened. When their hats bumped, he took them both off and wrapped himself in the blanket with her. "This is nice," he said with a twinkle in his eye. "All alone in the wilderness with a beautiful woman."

She drew him back to her, her lips hungry for the lush taste of his below the thick mustache, her tongue longing for the dance he had shown her. With a murmured sound of pleasure, he leaned her against the tree and pressed his long body into hers. With one hand he cupped the back of her head and Heather found herself imitating his gesture, burying her fingers in his hair. An unspoken shout of joy echoed through her, its vibrations singing with fluted notes through her nerves. The sense of destiny that had preceded her playing the steel-mill sonata, then had preceded Ben's entering her dressing room afterward, now returned full force. Fate had led them to this secluded grove, had led her into the arms of Ben Shaw; and she didn't intend to deny what fate had planned.

She dropped her hands to the buttons of his heavy coat and released them, and her mouth left his to trail down the scented path of his neck to the rise of his collarbone. Ben went utterly still for a moment, and when she undid the buttons of his shirt so that she could taste the crisp hair lightly covering his lean chest, he made a low noise. He brought his hands to her face and claimed her mouth with a hunger that jolted her simmering desire for him into a full-blown passion. With movements bordering on violence, he devoured her mouth, pressing his thumbs into her chin, and his fingers about her ears. The blanket fell away from them, forgotten.

She grasped the lapels of his coat as dizziness invaded her, a rush of emotion so intense that she could think of nothing beyond this cove in the trees and his lips upon her own. When his hands left her face to tear at the buttons of her coat, Heather pulled his body close to hers. Ben caught her wrists and pushed them down, pressing himself into her for a brief instant before finding her buttons again. With impatience he pushed the coat from her shoulders, his tongue thrusting and parrying with her own in an expert and unceasing dance. His tongue slid forward to just tip hers teasingly, then plunged hard, over and over, until Heather moaned at the symbolism of his movements. Again she lifted her hands to his chest to touch the blazing heat of his bare skin.

Ben breathed her name, his voice somewhere between a sigh and a groan. He pushed her away for a single moment, taking hold of her sweater at its hem and slowly drawing it over her head. As he lifted the material, Heather raised her hands and her breath came in short, shallow gasps as the cool air circled each inch he exposed—first her stomach, her ribs, and then her small unfettered breasts. At last he pulled the sweater free and flung it aside. "My God, you're beautiful," he whispered. His eyes blazed as he viewed her naked torso, covered with her streaming, tousled hair. Heather felt like the elfin queen he'd so often compared her to, as alluring as Helen of Troy. She raised her eyes and shook her head slightly to send her hair swirling over the peaks of her breasts, then held out her arms. "I've never had my clothes off outside before," she said softly. "I never knew it would feel so wonderful."

And he was glorious, as well. His unruly dark hair had been thoroughly disheveled by her raking fingers, and his eyes were black with hunger as he reached out to touch her over the small space separating them. A teasing light glowed in his face as he grasped her shoulders beneath her curtain of hair. He stepped up to her, seeming suddenly huge and overwhelmingly masculine. Against her thigh his manhood raged and as he eased closer yet, gently pushing her back against the rough bark of the pine, she knew that whatever coquettish game she could dream up, he could go her one better. When the crisp hairs covering his chest brushed against her breasts, pushing the satiny covering of her hair away, she knew she'd already lost. His gaze held hers, sultry and teasing and warm, and he moved infinitesimally back and forth against her naked chest, creating an explosion of heat in her middle. Fleetingly she wondered how he could remain so completely controlled. He dipped his head to murmur against her lips. "You're a nymph," he said, nibbling her mouth with tiny nips. "I can't let you go this time. But you don't really want me to, do you?"

She arched against him, straining for more contact, and something in his armor broke for an instant. He grasped her waist, the fingers digging almost painfully into her flesh, and his full mouth closed on hers in something close to desperation.

Suddenly he stooped to pick up discarded clothing and the blanket, which he wrapped around her shoulders. Dismayed, Heather thought she was about to be rebuffed again. Instead, he swept her up into his arms. "I can't enjoy you the way I want to here," he murmured, and helped her onto the horse. He jumped on behind and nickered to Buffalo, who turned to head out of the woods.

Heather felt dizzy when Ben's hands encircled her beneath the blanket. It seemed somehow delightfully forbidden to be almost naked under the blanket, anyway. To be astride the horse in the deep, silent snowfall added to her building desire in a way she would never have believed possible. She relaxed into Ben and laughed. "This is wonderful," she said softly.

His hands ascended her body beneath the blanket, the tips of his fingers cutting a freezing-hot trail. At the barrier of her arms holding the blanket, he paused, his molten mouth falling on her neck. "I want you to feel the snow on your naked breasts," he whispered. "I want the snow to melt on all that heat." His tongue teased up her neck. "And then I want to sip it all away."

She swallowed, dry mouthed at the reaction his words created. "What if someone sees?"

"I own a hundred acres—every inch of it fenced." He hugged her from behind. "It's okay, Heather. I'm playing with you. I can't quite believe you've never been naked outside before." He straightened a little, pulling his hands from beneath the blanket. "Hold on to it. I'm just going to pull it off your shoulders a little bit."

Heather complied, clutching for dear life to the blanket covering her breasts as he slipped it off her shoulders. A huge snowflake dropped to the hollow of her throat, another touched her collarbone. She leaned into Ben, letting her head fall back at his urging, and the snow fell on her exposed neck.

"I got one," he murmured, licking a cold flake away with his tongue. He slid his hands over her arms, enfolded her waist and pulled her closer still on the gently undulating back of the walking horse. Against her she felt his hardness and shivered at the thought of it—at the thought of him. "Oh, Ben," she breathed.

"I've never known anyone like you," he whispered against her ear.

Her joy rippled through her. This moment was unique in all of history; as unique as the snowflakes melting on her shoulders, as individual as her compositions, which couldn't be given life by anyone except her—just as she couldn't have been given this new lease on life by anyone except Ben. All the exuberance she'd felt upon the overwhelmingly positive acceptance of the "Steel Mill Sonata" now flooded through her again, heightened and enhanced by the man who held her. In a rush of full pleasure, she let go of the blanket and whooped. The snowflakes danced on her breasts and her outflung arms.

Ben made a sound behind her and his lips came down upon her shoulder at the same time his hands reverently reached up to stroke her breasts. His palms were hot—a heady contrast to the icy snow. The consuming hunger she'd known since meeting him broke free beyond any recalling. She moved her hands to his thighs—hard beneath the jeans—and clawed the cloth with her nails in her urgency to touch the flesh below. He played his fingers over her nipples, rolling and plucking them as expertly as Heather had ever played the guitar. He tenderly sucked the sensitive places at the nape of her neck and lashed her ear with his tongue. Boldly, Heather slid her hands up his thighs and heard his moan as she teased close to his arousal.

How they reached the barn at all would be a source of wonder later. In those moments, both were too grateful for its shelter to pause and question. Ben slid off Buffalo and pulled Heather into his arms, crushing her against him, bare chest to bare breast, his mouth covering hers with violent need. Somehow they'd made it inside the barn, to a bed of fragrant hay.

Ben urgently stripped off his coat and spread it out for them. He eased Heather to the ground where she lay suspended in the prelude of a symphony that had just begun to echo within her, watching as Ben stripped off his shirt. His supple torso was tawny and sleekly muscular; the dark curls of his head echoed over the lean lines of his chest. Heather held out her arms in supplication, and the first movement began as he came to her.

"I've imagined this a hundred times," he whispered as he took her in his arms. He lowered his head to close his mouth upon first one nipple and then the other, his tongue circling wider and wider until he had tasted every inch of the soft curves.

Heather heard violins take up the sound the flutes had begun in her veins as his mouth and hands played over her. He tasted the lengths of her arms, pausing at the vulnerable flesh of her inner elbow, drew shapes with his mouth upon her belly, slid her jeans from her body and tasted, too, that guarded center. Before she could be completely lost in the building symphonic sound, she grasped his shoulders and moved upon him to begin the second movement.

She'd never been a bold or imaginative lover, but now the music led her. She trailed the sweet and painful kisses over uncharted places of his body and traced the geography of his burning skin with her fingertips. The violins began a frantic whirr; the drums beat a slow backbeat, growing ever-so-faintly louder. Her breath began to heave in and out of her lungs until Ben could stand no more. With a hoarse curse, he crushed her to him, taking her mouth, his naked length glorious against her.

There was no pause now for play. Their desire was too sharp, too raw. Lips bruised, tongues tangled, hands grasped and stroked and explored, throats uttered groans and murmurs and gasps. The flutes and horns and violins crescendoed to a roar, with the drums crashing behind.

At last Ben moved above her and all time paused as their gazes locked. Reaching gracefully into his coat pocket, he whispered, "I figured you wouldn't have thought of this, so I took the liberty..."

"Thank you," she whispered, touched by his thoughtfulness.

When he finally plunged, the music commenced again, stronger and louder as he thrust with velvet and iron until Heather cried out, her head thrown back as she died and was reborn in a cataclysmic explosion. No longer could Ben tease and play and pull away. He, too, was drawn into the vortex to emerge, at the end, a different man.

Chapter Nine

It was nearly dusk when Heather awoke from a lazy doze to find Ben curled around her back. His head rested against her shoulder and one hand circled her waist protectively. Sensing her movement, he asked, "How about a shower, gorgeous?"

She shifted to look at him. "Are you coming with me?" After the first of their passion had spent itself, they'd returned to the house, to this room, where they had lingeringly discovered one another's secrets, making love with abandon, energetically and playfully.

"You better believe it."

They showered together, soaping each other and teasing and laughing, so sated from the afternoon's

luxurious mutual explorations that they even managed to get dressed. They made sandwiches of corned
beef and mustard, and shared mugs of hot chocolate
in the growing twilight of the comfortable kitchen.

"I imagine John should be back here pretty soon,"
Ben said, and raised an eyebrow in reluctant ac-
knowledgement of a world beyond the two of them.

"Real life must return, I suppose," Heather observed. She savored the salty flavor of her sandwich
and sighed. "I hate to see it happen."

"You don't have to go, you know." Ben reached
over the table to twine his long fingers with hers. His
brown eyes were sober and sweetly coercive. "We
could snuggle and watch TV, or maybe you could play
the guitar for me."

"I don't have my guitar with me."

"I've got one. It has metal strings, but it plays."

She cut him a suggestive glance. "What will you do
for me if I play the guitar for you?"

He laughed, showing his even teeth below the thick
mustache. "Whatever you want."

"I might be persuaded." The truth was, she had
nothing pressing to do and no desire to leave this
magical enclave. Her spirit soared from the shower of
healing water he'd poured upon her. She felt cleansed
and refreshed, tingly and glowy—even sexy and
beautiful. Every time her glance landed on Ben's rugged, sun-lined face within its frame of black hair, she
could scarcely believe her good fortune and couldn't
accept that he seemed to feel the same way about her.

Now his eyes leaped with the dancing humor she'd grown so fond of. "Name it."

She grinned. "Show me your office, Mr. Shaw— where all those books are created."

"Ah, a groupie. I knew it," he said with mock disappointment. "You want me to put on my spurs and whip, too?"

Heather couldn't resist the double entendre. A laugh gurgled in her chest. "That might be interesting, indeed, Mr. Shaw."

"Wench." He stood. "C'mon. You can bring your sandwich."

His limp, which Heather had rarely noticed since the train journey, was rather pronounced tonight and she noted he used the wall for support. As playfully as possible, she took his arm. "May I escort you, sir?"

The glance he threw her way was grateful, yet wry, as if he acknowledged both her recognition of his limp and her attempt to spare his pride.

He led the way to the back of the house to a room obviously added on at one time or another. Three walls were lined with windows. The last light of day glowed over a dark line of mountain peaks rising like a jagged curtain along the horizon.

Ben flipped on a lamp. "As you can see, I'm not the most organized housekeeper in the world. I don't often entertain visitors here."

Heather suddenly wondered if she was intruding. "Do you mind bringing me here?"

"Heck, no. It kind of makes me feel good, to tell you the truth." He glanced around the room, as if viewing it through her eyes. "Not much to it."

That was hardly true, Heather thought, as she drank in the essence of the office. A simple desk furnished with a typewriter was pushed against one wall and a neat stack of paper sat beside it, with a battered dictionary acting as paperweight. There the neatness ended. Papers and books were piled against filing cabinets, and notes were pinned up hurry-scurry over a corkboard. In one corner sat an overstuffed chair and ottoman next to a pine table with an overflowing ashtray. "Seems like it ought to be against the law to smoke in here," Heather commented, gesturing.

He looked up from a flaring match, smiling guiltily as he exhaled. "It's automatic. Everything in here's coated with six inches of tar."

Heather made a face and finished her examination. On the wall without windows was a series of framed magazine covers and book jackets; and whatever he said about tar, each showed evidence of recent dusting. Impulsively she turned. "Why do you act so casually about what you write?"

He squinted against the smoke of his cigarette, his stance automatically and unconsciously defensive. "I don't know what you mean."

"Yes, you do." She cocked her head. "Every time it comes up, you sort of shrug it off like it's a game. It can't be—not the way you write."

Ben held her gaze without speaking for a moment. "Something like the way you hide your music?"

"I'm not as talented as you are. I'm really mediocre as a musician."

Ben sank into the desk chair. "Well, I can't speak for the excellence of your playing. It impresses me because I can't do it. But if that composition you performed on the steel mill is any indication of your talent as a composer, you're the next Segovia."

At the mention of the steel-mill piece, Heather felt something tug at her memory. She frowned for a moment, then brushed it away. "No way. That piece was just luck—"

She broke off in a flush of overwhelming horror. With widened eyes, she scanned the room for a calendar. "Oh, my God. What's the date today?" A thudding sickness enveloped her belly and every good emotion she'd been feeling sank straight through the floor.

Ben stood up. "What is it?"

Heather desperately tried to stem the flood of panic in her chest. Maybe she'd miscounted. Her eyes found a small bank calendar on the wall just above the desk. Sunday, November 9. A wave of weakness smashed her knees and she nearly buckled before Ben's strong grip snagged her arm. The weight pulled on his bad leg and both of them nearly fell.

"Sit down before we both kill ourselves," he said harshly.

Heather's hands were trembling so badly she had to force them together on her lap. "James died today," she whispered, aghast all over again at the realization of how she'd spent this anniversary. Cold shame racked her spine.

"Heather, it was three years ago." He knelt in front of her. "Don't let it get to you."

"How can you say that?"

"People die. Somebody dies on every day of the calendar."

It was the same argument she'd heard a thousand times from Mike, and she jumped up. "Go ahead and tell me I'm going to see this date once a year for the rest of my life," she replied with a shaking voice. "Go ahead and tell me you can't wall yourself off because someone dies." Now anger mixed with the violence of her reaction and the whole of her internal organs seemed to tremble and flame all at once.

Ben looked at her, his hands on his hips. "That's exactly what I was going to say."

"Well, James didn't just *die*," she proclaimed sharply.

He didn't look shocked or curious or any of the other things she expected. He simply nodded. "I know." There was a slight edge of impatience in his tone. "He shot himself. I'm sure it was gruesome and horrible and ugly. I'm sorry you had to find him."

"How did you know I found him? Did Mike fill you in on all the gory details?" Her chest felt as if it would explode. She had to get out of there, had to get back to town.

A pulse jumped in his jaw. "I already knew most of it, Heather. Mike just plugged the gaps."

The knowledge that he'd learned the ugly secrets of James's death made her feel invaded. Her eyes narrowed. "Did Mike also tell you that I made him do it?"

"Damn it, woman, what are you talking about?" Ben's voice rose. "James was always weak."

She slapped him hard. "How dare you!"

When she pulled back for a second hit, he grabbed her arms in a steely grip, his own temper blazing. "I dare because I can't stand to see you wasting yourself over somebody who didn't deserve you." He dragged her, fighting and kicking, toward the window.

"You have no right to make those judgments," she shrieked.

"He's dead, Heather!" His nearly black eyes blazed. He threw open a window, one hand bruisingly holding her arm. He grabbed a handful of snow and pressed it to her neck. "You feel that? That means you're alive." His lips took hers, violent and hot and mindless, then released them. "That means I am."

With an abruptness that nearly sent her sprawling, he released her. "Now, if you want to go lie with a dead man, you go ahead."

Confused and utterly unable to think, Heather stood in the center of the room, gasping. She watched as Ben crossed the floor and scrabled in a desk drawer. He threw her a ring of keys. "My car's out-side. Go ahead. I surely won't hold you here against your will."

For the briefest, longest moment, she hesitated. Icy snow slid into the collar of her shirt. Ben's eyes bored into the depths of her soul. Her chest ached and her eyes burned and her lips felt battered. As she bent to pick up the keys that had landed at her feet, a pull of sore muscles reminded her of the way she'd spent the day, and a sharply focused picture of James, as big as a movie close-up, blotted everything else from her mind.

In mortification, she fled outside, barely hearing Ben's harsh curse behind her.

The snow had ceased, but the roads were snow-packed and probably icy. Heather gazed in dismay at the open expanse of white, and her fear of bad roads nearly cut through the turmoil of shame and humili-ation she felt. For one brief second, she thought of calling a cab, but the thought of returning to the house, to the snapping judgment of Ben's eyes, to his cutting words, then waiting a solid hour for the cab, decided her. She flung open the car door.

He had no right to talk about James like that, she thought furiously as she pumped the accelerator and cranked the ignition. Before the war, James had planned to enter the priesthood—not the vocation of a weak man; only that of a sensitive one.

The car was obviously well maintained, for the en-gine caught and held immediately. Heather shivered, coatless, while it warmed up. She wouldn't even risk going back for her coat.

As it turned out, she didn't have to. Ben appeared on the porch, his features unyielding and distant. Without even descending the steps, he tossed the coat onto the hood of the car and went back inside. The abrupt gesture, so angry and disdainful, sent a sharp pain through Heather's middle, as real as if he'd punched her. Some portion of her whirling brain screamed a half-formed protest as she climbed out of the car to shake off the coat and put it on. The door to the cabin was shut tight and Heather thought of the warmth beyond, of the sandwich she hadn't finished and the fire they might have had later.

Heavy, thudding guilt intervened. If James had died in a car accident, by now she would be able to enjoy the loving company Ben offered; she would be free to love him in return. Unfortunately, James had killed himself because his wife couldn't deal with the ugly realities of his war days; because she'd been horrified at confessions he had laboriously made—after years of knowing her; after Heather had *begged* to share his past with him.

Her misery was so intense as she drove back to Pueblo that she drove automatically over roads that indeed were very slick. Ben had good tires on the front-wheel-drive import and it hugged the road with secure control. Heather's mind wandered bleakly over the unbroken white of the landscape, caught in a familiar and hated cycle of memories. As night fell, her

mood dipped even further. She hadn't even made it to
James's grave on the anniversary of his death, she be-
rated herself. Instead, she'd spent the day wrapped in
heedless passion, laughing and playing with Ben like
a liberated virgin, mindless and free.

But she wasn't free, and she would never be so
again. Her sheltered and protected childhood hadn't
prepared her for the depth and power of another person's pain. She'd ruined one life with her narrow
background, and Ben deserved someone stronger.

She made it home in just under an hour. The house
was dark, and loomed like a haunted castle before her,
almost leering with an obscene aura of tragedy. For a
long time, Heather couldn't bear to go inside. She sat
in the driveway with her hands wrapped around the
steering wheel, staring at the building's cold facade. *I
hate this house,* she thought suddenly. She'd always
hated it—the stolidness and lack of imagination and
air and light. On winter mornings, the living room was
so dark it felt like a cave thanks to heavy pines that
blocked what little light there was. The flowers grew
in precise, ordered rows that were so unlike nature they
looked unreal.

Everything she hated about it, James had loved.
He'd worshiped order and solidity, which was one
thing about him Heather didn't miss. He'd hated the
house to fall into disorder, and like her family, had
wanted meals at the same time every day, to the point
of driving her crazy. He would have been well suited
to a scholarly life, living behind the bricked walls of a

secluded monastery. The thing was, Heather thought, no such place existed anywhere that she knew of. The priests and nuns of her childhood had been ordinary men and women, involved in the community and the schools and with people. James wouldn't have done well trying to live that sort of life.

With a ripping, searing sense of justice, she realized she hated James as much as she hated the house. She hated him for cheating her and making her feel so rotten. He hadn't even left a note—just the gory remains of his act where she would be sure to find them.

She got out of the car heavily. Neither hating the house nor hating James were new emotions. They were a regular part of this yearly ritual. With a deep sigh, she unlocked her door and prepared to fight the ghosts of this night's coming.

Ben's first impulse was to drink a bottle of whatever he could get his hands on and then rip the house to pieces. Ten years ago, that's exactly what he would have done. He contented himself with a curse and a fist slammed into a wall. The gesture brought a wry grin to his face. *Can't even get properly mad, man.* He grimaced when he recalled the childish toss of her coat onto the hood of the car. That had been about on a par with his behavior in his earlier years.

He'd never hit a woman in his life—discounting his sisters, who hit back just as hard. But as he'd watched Heather shrink from the voluptuously alive woman who'd made love with him with the abandon of a magnificent lioness into the haunted, confused little girl she'd become within seconds, he'd *wanted* to hit her—not to hurt her, but to wake her up to her real life which was speeding past her with the same fury his own life had bypassed him while he'd hidden from his own ghosts.

His running had taken place in dozens of bars in the arms of dozens of women. His ghost had been the self he'd wanted to be, the man who'd made crowds roar furiously when he leaped onto the back of a bucking bronco.

Like James, Ben had also run from the nightmare of combat—the same in all wars, if what his father said about the Pacific was anything to judge by. Whoever kept thinking up these wars sure didn't have to fire the rifles. Human beings weren't cut out for that rot—an opinion that slipped into his novels over and over and over again.

He lit a cigarette and watched darkness fall over the mountain. He couldn't help Heather. She had to find out for herself that she was the only one who could live her life. That knowledge squeezed his heart painfully, but it couldn't touch the thrumming love he felt for her. Sometimes loving meant stepping back to let people live their own lives, complete with mistakes.

A huge swell of regret filled his lungs. It was the same old story: something so good wrapped in something so bad—the strange pattern of his life. He should have known to be suspicious of his seemingly wondrous fortune; should have kept his heart out of the whole thing.

But even as he thought it, he knew it would have been impossible. For Heather was the woman of his dreams, in spite of the insecurities that kept her clinging to a grief that should have been put to rest ages ago. She was a woman capable of great emotion, capable of expressing those emotions—through her music if nowhere else—and capable, too, of nurturing; a woman capable of accepting and reveling in the deep passion he'd conceived for her, a passion that would last until the end of his days.

A huge well of unexpressed feeling pushed at his chest. There was one way to expel it if he wasn't going to drown in a bottle. He stubbed out his cigarette and went to his office. A little girl had a story to finish.

The graveyard depressed Heather—doubly so with the bitterly cold weather that had settled in overnight. It was an obligatory visit. She felt nothing at all when she laid the wreath of flowers on James's grave with the others that had been placed there yesterday. The right day. What must Mike and his mother have thought of her?

She'd canceled all her classes and appointments for the day. For one, her head ached and her eyes were swollen. Even her neck was stiff from a virulent cold that had set in as she'd fitfully tossed and turned through the night. She knew it was stress, but that didn't make it any easier to bear. It had taken every bit of her strength to get dressed, buy the flowers and drive to the graveyard. Now she had to trade Ben's car for her own, which she'd left at the arts center the night he'd picked her up.

The weather matched her grim mood. None of the enchanting snowflakes that had created such a magical mood in the forest yesterday fell now. A pewter-colored sky grayed the old buildings downtown, and traffic had dirtied the snow along the sides of the streets. Even the sight of the steel mill—its rounded fingers reaching into the sky with dark symmetry—didn't cheer her. She thought of the day three years ago when she'd finished her composition instead of the thrill of the audience's ardent response to it Saturday night.

She left Ben's car at the center and drove to Mike's house, hoping to find him home for lunch. Although she knew where his shop was located, she hated to bother him there, and there was no guarantee of the kinds of comments his men would make. She was absolutely not in a state of mind to be gracious about lewd remarks.

Ellen, dressed in a flowing blouse and worn jeans, answered the door. "Hi, Heather. You look awful."

Heather frowned and followed Ellen in. "Thank you very much. Is your husband here?"

"You don't sound very good, either. Come on in the kitchen and let me make you a cup of tea. Mike should be here any time."

In the kitchen Ellen bustled about, putting water on for tea. "I guess you must feel pretty good about yourself, eh?" she asked.

"Frankly," Heather replied, "I've got such a rotten cold, the whole world looks like a mine shaft at the moment."

Ellen gave her a motherly look and pressed a hand to Heather's forehead. "No fever, but your eyes are red." Her wide blue eyes narrowed. "Did you spend the night crying or something? I know it was James's anniversary yesterday."

"No, I didn't cry." She'd been too miserable for tears. They never seemed to help anything, anyway. "I'm just stressed out, I guess. I never get sick unless I am."

"Good things coming too fast can be as hard as bad things, too, you know."

"What good things?"

Ellen laughed incredulously. "The rave reviews of your steel-mill piece, for one thing. That gorgeous hunk of male you spent the weekend with, for another. Those are a couple of things I'd kick up my heels over."

Before Heather could answer, the roar of a Harley-Davidson in the driveway signaled Mike's arrival, and a minute later, he bounded into the kitchen. "Hello, baby," he greeted, sweeping Heather in a bear hug. "You've made both of us famous."

"What?"

With a smug grin, he let her go to kiss Ellen. "I forgot you were hidden away in loverland all weekend. Guess you haven't seen yesterday's paper?"

"No."

Mike dipped under a pile of newspapers on the table and withdrew the life-style section with a flourish. In a surprisingly good photograph, Heather was depicted playing her guitar. Her braid fell over one shoulder, glistening like a strand of jewels against the dark velvet of her costume. "Newcomer Captures Mill Life" the headline read. Heather gaped. "How did this happen?"

"I did it," Mike admitted with a grin. "When Tom told me you'd given him that piece, and then told me how great it was, I talked him into getting you to play it and I called Joe at *The Chieftain*." His dark blond curls bounced as he straightened triumphantly. "He was impressed, to say the least."

Heather stared at him, struggling with several conflicting emotions. "I can't believe you would be so devious," she commented finally.

"There's more."

"Pray tell," Heather inquired dryly.

"I recorded it, and the tape is on its way to a producer Joe recommended."

Heather jumped up, furious. The motion sent a pounding to her clouded head and she pressed a chilly-fingered hand to her eye. "You had no right to do that without my permission."

Ellen backed off toward the stove. "I told you she wouldn't be happy about that."

Mike crossed his arms, his tattoos bulging over massive muscles. His face was set in a stubborn expression, his eyes as revealing as glass. "You don't have enough confidence in yourself, Heather. If I hadn't done it, you never would have."

"That doesn't give you the right to meddle in my life. Who do you think you are?"

"I'm the only brother you ever had—maybe the only relative who ever cared enough about you to make you try."

Heather sighed, suddenly exhausted and dangerously close to tears. She sank back into the chair. "All right." She sighed. "We'll just wait and see what happens. It can't hurt anything, I guess."

Ellen brought her a cup of tea and with extreme gentleness, kissed the top of Heather's head. "We love you, sweetie. I hope you know that."

Touched, Heather glanced up. "I know. Thank you." She sipped the strong, hot tea for courage and looked at Mike. "I came by to ask you a favor."

"Shoot."

"I drove Ben's car down here yesterday, and I left it at the arts center. I wonder if you would give him his keys?"

Mike pressed his lips together. "Sorry, Heather. I can't do that."

His refusal was like a shock of cold water. "Why?"

"Because it's time you stopped hiding. I've played along with this game longer than I should have already, and I'm not doing it anymore."

"What makes you think I'm hiding?"

"If you weren't, you'd give him the keys yourself."

The logic was irrefutable. "We had a fight, and I don't feel comfortable seeing him right now."

Mike shrugged. "You'll have to find someone else to be your intermediary, then."

"Thanks ever so much," Heather replied stiffly, rising to her feet. "I'll see myself out."

As she brushed past Mike, he shot his arm out and grabbed hers. "Take care of yourself, honey," he said.

She shook herself free. "No problem."

With her head whirling and pounding, Heather drove back home and once there, dived directly into bed, covering her face with the pillows. Here some cold medicine she'd ingested proved to be a friend rather than an enemy, for she fell directly into sleep, a sleep during which nothing could touch her.

Unfortunately the respite didn't last long. After three hours of gloriously numbed sleep, Heather was awakened by the insistent ringing of the doorbell. Groggily she made her way to the door and peered through the peephole. Tom stood in its warped view. Heather blinked. Monday, she remembered, was the day she'd told him to come by. "Just a minute," she called, then rushed to the bathroom to brush her hair and splash cold water on her face. As she bent over the sink, her head throbbed malevolently and she coughed.

She opened the door to Tom and a small young woman who accompanied him. They both smiled and Heather felt a twinge of guilt for her inhospitable sentiments. "Hello," she greeted as warmly as she could manage.

"Oh, you sound like you've got a bad cold," Tom said with a frown. "Should we come back another time?"

"No, please come in." She brushed her hair away from her face and led them inside. "Can I get you a cup of tea? I was just about to make a pot."

"Sure." Tom looped an affectionate arm around the girl at his side. "I want you to meet my fiancée, Helen."

The girl was barely twenty, but her pale eyes showed knowledge beyond her years. Her smile was friendly but reserved. "I've heard a lot about you, Heather."

"Nothing bad, I hope."

"Hardly. He raves about you all the time." She looked up at Tom with tenderness. "You've really brought him out of his shell."

Heather padded barefoot into the kitchen to start a pot of water boiling and returned to the others. "So, what's the word?"

Tom cleared his throat and sat forward on the couch. "I have an audition for Professor Caine on Thursday afternoon." The color that crept up his cheeks at nervous moments now inched toward his eyes. "When I told them you insisted I come talk to them, they were real impressed."

Heather smiled. "Who did you talk to today?"

"Dr. Jacobs?" He said the name as if he were unsure it was the right one. "Short man with long white hair?"

"That's him. He's very eccentric but a lot of fun. You'll take all your basic classes from him."

"If I get in."

"You will." She noted the trembling of his fingers. "Did you find out about taking your GED?"

He nodded. "They have a class I can take to help prepare for it, too."

"Good." The teakettle whistled and Heather jumped. "I have quite a few kinds of tea. Would you like to choose, or shall I surprise you?"

"Surprise us," Helen said. "I'm sure you know more than we do about it." She stood. "Can I help you with something?"

"I'll let you bring in the cream and sugar."

As Heather readied the pot, choosing a flowery Darjeeling, she realized she felt better. She still had the cold, of course, but her gloom had lifted. James—and Ben—seemed like distant specters, like people she'd read about in a book. *Live for the moment,* she thought with an ironic twist to her lips, *and the days will take care of themselves.*

The three chatted easily over the tea. Then Helen suggested Tom get his guitar from the car. He was reluctant at first, but with some coaxing was persuaded to fetch it.

When he returned, Heather gave him a severe look. "I didn't give you my steel-mill piece so that you could show it to my brother-in-law, by the way."

"Not consciously," Tom replied with a grin.

She'd expected him to at least look ashamed. When he didn't, she had to wonder if there wasn't some truth to his words. Maybe her subconscious *was* healthier than her everyday mind. "Well, let's hear it. Have you learned it?"

"Some." He laboriously picked out the major themes. "It's not the simplest thing to play, with those double leads."

"I wanted it to work on two levels. With two guitars, they could be separated."

"I guess they can."

"What are you going to play for the audition?"

"I was thinking about the last piece you gave me—the one I played in class that day."

She nodded, and leaning over her guitar, made a note on an envelope on the table. "I also think you should brush up on the Mozart I taught you near the first of the year."

For an hour they reviewed and played portions of the two compositions and discussed the merits of several others before settling on a third, modern-blues piece that showcased Tom's acute interpretation of mood.

"Thanks, Heather," Tom said, standing to leave. "I really appreciate your help."

"No problem. In fact," she blurted out, suddenly seeing a way to fill some of the yawning hours of the week, "if you like, we can rehearse an hour or two every day until Thursday."

Although the move had been made selfishly, Heather was gratified by the sudden blaze of appreciation in Tom's eyes. "That'd be great."

"You're welcome to come along, Helen," Heather added.

The girl smiled but shook her head. "I think Tom will practice more seriously if I'm not here. I'll stay home this week, but I hope to see you again."

"Anytime."

She saw them out, then, faced with the deep silence of the house, fed her pets, and rationalizing that colds were the body's bid for rest, went back to bed. At nine she awoke, took another cold tablet and slept through the night. If the phone rang, she didn't hear it.

Chapter Ten

Tuesday morning, Heather's phone *did* ring, but it wasn't Ben asking about his car. Instead, the man who'd spoken to her about playing in his club phoned to see if she was still interested. Arrangements were made for her to come in Thursday to examine the area and talk in-depth about the terms of her employment. It was more money than Heather had ever made playing anything, and in spite of her cold, she was pleased.

When she hung up, she paused with her hand on the telephone. She had to make arrangements for the return of Ben's car. Biting her lip, she dialed the numbers quickly, before she could change her mind.

"Hello?" It wasn't Ben on the other end of the line, and she felt a surge of relief.

"Hello. This is Heather Scarborough and I have Ben's car. I'd like to make arrangements to get it back to him."

"Just a minute."

Before Heather could utter a word of protest, John had laid the phone down. For one cowardly second, she considered just hanging up and leaving them to deal with the question of the car. But the courtesy that had been drilled into her for eighteen years wouldn't allow her to do it. She'd borrowed the car. It was her responsibility to see that it was properly returned.

Ben's voice, cool and distant, came through the line this time. "Heather."

"Yes."

"Can you drive it up here? John will take you back."

Her stomach plummeted. Why couldn't they be in a real city, she thought with irritation, where cabs were as common as pennies? People here considered them extravagant and slightly suspicious—a throwback, she supposed, to the hard-chiseled self-reliance of the settlers of the Old West.

Ben seemed to sense her hesitation. "Don't worry," he added, "I won't be anywhere in sight."

It seemed impossible that this was the same man who'd held her so lovingly on Sunday afternoon, the same man whose voice had whispered loving words. This voice held no husky undercurrent of seduction.

STRANGERS ON A TRAIN

This voice was hard and cold—even a touch exasperated. It reminded her of the night he'd had his seizure in her house and abruptly shut her out. Again Heather thought of James—James in one of his bad moods—and the protective shield she'd erected against Ben was reinforced with another layer. She could only really be hurt if she allowed someone to get close to her. "It isn't necessary for you to avoid me. I'll bring the car this afternoon, if that's a satisfactory arrangement for you two."

"I wasn't avoiding *you*, lady."

"Point taken," she replied coldly. "I have lessons this morning. Will two o'clock be all right?"

"Fine."

As she hung up the phone the second time, her elation was gone. Her headache thumped heavily against the back of her skull and she coughed, summoning a requisite amount of self-pity; if she had to return his silly car today, she wouldn't even be able to take her cold tablets. But at least it would be over then. She wouldn't have to think of Ben Shaw anymore—or of how close she had come to falling in love again.

When Ben hung up, he threw his pencil across the room, swearing more violently than he had in years.

John moved the dishes from lunch and joked, "I like this set. If you want to break plates, let me get you the Goodwill stuff."

"Oh, hell, man. This woman is driving me crazy."

"I didn't notice."

Ben narrowed his eyes. "You're the one who does all the falling in love. What would you do in a case like this?"

"A case like what?"

"She thinks she owes her dead husband something."

John pursed his lips. "Maybe just let her work it out."

It was essentially the same advice Ben had given himself on Sunday, but it wasn't any easier to swallow from John. He rubbed his face. "I've even finished this novel. I feel at loose ends."

"You've done the rewrite, too?"

Ben wiggled his nose as he lit a cigarette. "It won't need much. This was one of the lucky ones. Some angel or something wrote it, not me."

"So, maybe you should go back to New York, take it to your agent and see a play or something."

Ben nodded. "That might work. At least it'll get me out of town for a week or two. I could go down to Virginia and see my sister when I'm done."

"You want me to make the arrangements?"

Ben warmed to the idea. Maybe he could even stay with his sister through Christmas. At least he would be out of temptation's way. And maybe by the time he got back, he could approach Heather again—they would have gotten over this infatuation. It would be done, either way. He couldn't sit in this house all winter and wait for her. That just wasn't his way.

To John's question, he answered, "Yeah. I'll leave as soon as you can get me a seat." He stood. "I don't want to see her when she comes."

"You got it."

By the time Heather started the thirty-mile drive to Beulah, her eyes were grainy, her nose was raw and her cough had deepened into a harsh barking. She kept telling herself she'd invited the cold to attack her so that she wouldn't have to deal with her emotions, but that didn't seem to lessen the severity of her symptoms at all.

It was a long, miserable drive, overlaid with dread. "Dear God," she prayed aloud, "if you love me at all, please let him be taking a shower or something when I get there."

But when she pulled up in front of the house and saw no sign of Ben, she felt a little tremor of disappointment. Oh, make up your mind, she thought irritably. She slammed the car door with more force than she'd intended.

Before she got to the porch, the same man who'd picked Ben up the night of his seizure appeared on the porch, slipping his arms into a heavy leather jacket. "Hi," he said.

Heather took a breath. "Hi."

"You ready?"

She nodded, giving him the keys and turning from the house to climb into the passenger seat. In front of her, through the windshield, she could see the wide-open field that led to Ben's forest grove. If she turned her face the slightest bit to the right, she would be able to see the edge of the barn, but she stared straight ahead. As it was, she was hard put to keep the earthy memories of Sunday afternoon at bay. As John started the car and guided it out of the circular driveway, she had a clear mental flash of Ben behind her on the horse, with the snow falling on her naked shoulders, and she couldn't resist a last glance at the house.

Only the blank windows returned her gaze, and Heather hunched into her seat.

All at once she admitted that she'd wanted to see him, had wanted a chance to explain her reactions on Sunday. She'd wanted to ease the terrible scene that had separated them.

On the heels of that thought came another: free or not, she loved him. The knowledge racked her like a vicious shaking from a brutal parent. Her feelings had crossed the line at some point, had deepened when she wasn't paying attention. Oh, God! she breathed silently. How could I have let this happen?

With quiet sympathy, John touched her hand between the seats, squeezed it once and let it go. After a moment he said, "I saw the article about you in the paper Sunday. I wish I could have heard that. My dad worked at the mill for thirty-five years."

Gratefully, Heather accepted his conversational lifeline. "What did he do?"

"He was a millwright."

"Tell me about him."

John willingly did just that, giving Heather a glimpse of a Pueblo flush with mill money twenty years before. The stories kept her from brooding on the trip back, and when John dropped her at the arts center, she paused. "Thank you," she said.

He seemed to understand she was thanking him for more than the ride, for with a sober nod he replied, "Chin up."

Later in the silence of her own house, Heather headed straight for the bathroom, swallowed her cold tablets and went to bed. She had never been sicker in her life.

Mike scrambled closer to the World War II Triumph motorcycle he was restoring, easing a bolt free with infinite patience. The socket slipped suddenly when his heel moved an inch in the gravel beneath his feet and his knuckles landed hard against a jutting, immovable shelf of metal. Snatching his fingers back, he swore violently and slammed the tool down. No matter how many times he did it, he never got used to the first searing pain of knuckles scraped raw.

"Mike."

He turned toward Tom's voice with irritation. "What is it?" The kid was nice and all, but he could show up at the worst times.

"I'm kinda worried about Heather. I thought you oughta know."

"Heather?" He stood up and looked at Tom. "What's wrong?"

He dipped his head, then looked back. "I don't know. She was supposed to meet me today, and I can't get her to answer the door."

Mike grimaced and shook his stinging fingers. "Hell, man, she's probably off with her boyfriend."

Tom shook his head stubbornly. "No, she wouldn't do that. She said she'd meet me."

Mike looked at him. Heather had been sick yesterday, he remembered. "She wouldn't answer the door?"

Tom drew himself up to his full height, standing straight for the first time in Mike's memory. "I think you oughta check on her, make sure she's okay."

Mike licked his lips and considered.

"Maybe she's sick or something," Tom added.

"Something." Mike nodded. "Thanks, Tom. I'll go by there."

"Good. I don't mean to interfere, you know, or anything like that."

"I know. I appreciate your coming over here. Thanks."

"See ya, then."

Mike wrapped his bleeding fingers with a clean rag and considered the dilemma set before him. Would he play knight and go see if he could rescue Heather from her dragons? Again?

He wanted to. He wanted to rage over to her house on his noisy Harley, then pound on her door and roar until she dragged herself out of bed. Then, he thought with satisfaction, he would shake her until her teeth rattled, until her numbed brain was shocked to life.

No. She needed a good shaking up, but not a physical one. And he didn't think he was the one to administer what she needed.

If he'd learned anything at all in Alcoholics Anonymous, it was that each person had the control of his or her own life. Pity didn't help somebody who was stuck in a ditch with mud in their eyes. You could toss them a cloth to wash the mud away, but they had to do the washing themselves.

For two years, he'd been acting as guard over his sister-in-law, effectively shielding her from any help she might have found within herself. It had been guilt and sorrow, he supposed. He'd worried about his little brother constantly after he'd returned from Vietnam, but at first Heather had seemed to really help James.

Mike had spent a lot of time since James's suicide wishing he'd been more alert to the signs that his brother wasn't facing his war memories well. His constant monitoring of Heather's terrible grief had been, in part, a way of making it up to his brother.

Now he saw that that, too, was a game. He wasn't giving Heather enough credit. Look at the way she'd managed her love life, he thought. For years, he'd been pushing every suitable candidate he could find at her, and she'd just as steadily ignored them—then gone out and found herself one hell of a decent man in Ben Shaw.

Ben was old enough to know what he was doing. He was patient, Mike thought. That would help. But even Ben wouldn't wait forever. What would happen to Heather then?

He quelled his urge to go to see her, after all. Heather had to fight her own dragons, be her own knight in shining armor. He had a hunch no one would be more surprised than she at the bang-up job she would do when she found no one was going to do it for her.

The vivid picture he imagined brought a smile to his face: Heather, her glorious hair spilling over the blue velvet gown she'd worn for *Twelfth Night*, swinging Excalibur with both hands, a grimace of fury on her face.

He wished he could be there to see it.

When Heather awoke, it was long past dark. Her mouth was dry and she was stiff from sleeping, but the heavy, banging headache was gone. Once she rose and stretched, she realized she felt better all over.

A lot better.

Gone were the runny nose, the scratchy throat and grainy eyes. Except for her deep thirst, it was almost as if she'd gone for a dip in a magical pool of healing water, to be instantly cured.

Propelled by her thirst, she went to the kitchen and drank two huge glasses of water, then automatically put the kettle on for tea. In the living room, Amadeus chirped with shrill notes. Heather smiled. "You missed me, didn't you baby?"

In his flurry of chirps was the plaintive answer. Heather released him, stroking his head and under his chin. Ordinarily aloof, Peter scooted toward her and she pet one bird with each hand. "I don't know what I'd do without you guys."

Her gaze fell on the digital clock on the stereo. The red numbers showed 9:09 p.m. and with a wince, she remembered Tom. "Excuse me, guys. I have to make a phone call."

First she dialed Mike to get the telephone number. When her brother-in-law came to the phone he said, "Where've you been?"

"What do you mean?" Heather asked, frowning at the tone of his voice. "I've been here, if it's any of your business."

"Well, hell. Tom came by here this afternoon worried about you because you didn't answer the door. Are you okay?"

"I'm fine," she answered. "I was sleeping off my cold."

"You sound a lot better."

"I am."

A brief pause stretched between them. "Are you still mad at me, Heather?"

She sighed. "No. You were right. I took the car back myself."

"And?"

"And nothing." She struggled to keep her voce neutral, but it sagged a little when she added, "I didn't even see him. His secretary drove me back."

"Does that bother you?"

Heather touched the bridge of her nose. "Mike, I just can't get involved with anyone yet. It's too hard. It's too frightening." She shook her hair away from her face, and before Mike could be sympathetic or irritated—neither of which she wanted to deal with—she said, "Why don't you give me Tom's phone number so that I can apologize?"

Mike gave her the number and she quickly ended the conversation. When she called Tom, he picked up the phone on the second ring.

"Hi, Tom. This is Heather. Did you come by this afternoon?"

"I did, but you didn't answer. Are you all right?"

"I'm fine. I just got up." She paused. "I'm really sorry I couldn't practice with you this afternoon."

"It's all right. I understand."

"I'll clear my schedule and we can spend the whole evening on practice tomorrow night, okay?"

"Sure." He sounded doubtful.

"I promise I'll answer the door this time," she said lightly, hoping to coax a chuckle from him, and was disappointed at her lack of success.

"I believe you," he replied solemnly.

"Are you feeling nervous?"